The Daughters of Time, Book 3

The Secrets of the Storm

C.S. Kjar

Editor: JoEllen Claypool
Cover Designed by jimmygibbs
Proofreading by John Buchanan and Julie Martin

Available in eBook and Paperback

ISBN-13: 978-0-9985897-8-7
ISBN-10: 0-9985897-8-0

https://cskjar.com

This book is dedicated to sisters everywhere. Whether sisters by blood or sisters by love, treasure your relationships. Go have fun!

Chapter 1

The gray dust on the moon's surface floated around Father Time's boots and the hem of his long cloak as he walked across the gray surface. Above him, the darkness of the universe held his attention. Planets, stars, galaxies, black holes, and gaseous clouds floated in limitless space. The harmonic music of the spheres filled the empty spaces between them. His favorite place spun on its axis overhead. Its white poles, blue water, and green land provided a colorful contrast against the blackness of the universe. A smile cracked his face as he watched everything running in synchronous accord.

"You seem pleased with yourself."

Father Time spun around to see who had interrupted his peaceful moment of introspection. There, in her leafy gown flowing down her body and across the lunar surface, stood Mother Nature. Her crown of calla lilies, white roses, and moonflowers framed her round face. Her thick, mossy hair was braided and fell over one shoulder. The tilt of her head and her hands on her hips signaled the tone of the impending conversation.

"Hello, Terra," he said with the same grit as moonscape sand. Their last conversation had turned bitter with her request to make summer seasons shorter so less of the ice cap would melt. He turned his back on her. "Won't your flowers wilt in this harsh, non-atmospheric sun?"

Terra gave a snort. "No, they won't, Chronos, but thanks for your nonexistent concern."

She was one of the few who called him by his given name. Coming off her tongue, it sounded like a squeaky spring in an ancient mattress. "Why are you here?"

"I found out your latest wife died recently. Why didn't you tell me about it? I would have sent my condolences."

With the toe of his boot, Chronos flicked up a small amount of dust and let it hang there, floating between the lunar surface and the earth. He gritted his teeth and tapped his fingertips against his thigh. Answering Terra's question about his beloved Frances wasn't hard, but her rebuttals to his statements would ruin his tranquility.

"My beloved Francis died peacefully five years ago. I cannot speak to why you didn't hear about it. I'm not in your social circle."

Terra huffed as she stomped around him. "I don't know why you insist on mixing with mortals. Their lives are so short, you hardly have time to be together. I told you more than five millennia ago we immortals need to stick together."

"I cannot direct where my heart takes me. Francis was precious to me, and you will not talk against her or my daughters." He moved away from the growing dust cloud Terra's gown was stirring up. If he left now, he'd be away from her, but he'd have to come back and remove their footprints from the lunar dust. Humans would return to the moon one day, and mysterious footprints would cause too many erroneous conjectures on how they got there.

Terra came up beside him, hooked her arm through his, and leaned her head on his shoulder. "I meant no disrespect for her or your daughters. I only mean we should be better friends." She tickled the edges of his beard. "I'm an immortal like you. I'm here for you. Together we could improve the universe, restore what's damaged, and fill it with good things."

2

Father Time pulled his arm away from her. "I'm sorry, Terra. I still grieve for my Francis."

"I'm not proposing marriage!" She tramped away, grumbling something about idiocy. "I'm talking about far greater things," she said with a viper's tongue.

A forced smile moved her face as she opened her arms and faced Earth. "Think of it, Chronos! What wonderous things we could do! Reversing time would allow me to heal the earth. I could bring back some of my children who are gone forever. I could purify the water, land, and skies so they are clean and fertile. Together we could heal this creation."

Father Time's eyes stayed on Earth, watching a continent slowly spin into the shadow of night. "What's done is done. Time moves forward. You cannot go back and change the past." He moved away from her but spoke loudly enough so that she'd hear. "You're right about one thing. We're immortals and we're stuck with each other. We should move beyond our past and be nicer to each other. We could talk more often, but alas, my duties keep me very busy. I can't help you save the earth, but perhaps there's a handsome wood nymph or hamadryad that might help you in your restoration efforts. They can help you more than I can."

In a whirlwind of moon dust, Mother Nature wheeled about to stand in from of him. "I need time to save the world, Chronos. You've got what I need. Time."

"Use wisely the time given to you," he said as he pulled his cloak around him. "Heal the earth, but don't ask me to turn back time because I won't."

"Then give me your magic clock."

He stood rooted to the spot. Of all the secrets he held, his magic clock was the most sacred. The clock held his secrets. It was the portal that allowed him to connect with the mortal world. Only with the clock could mortals alter time and call him and others. Only his most trusted wives and children had access to it, and its secrets would die with them. He thought no one else knew about it. This new revelation from Terra frightened him.

He turned slowly to face Terra, wondering which of his daughters had let their secret slip. "How do you know about the clock?"

Terra looked at her green nails, polished one with a fingertip, then folded her hands. "Little children have such a hard time keeping secrets. Seems one of your granddaughters saw her grandmother coming out of a clock after she died. Is that true?"

The vacuum of space hovered between them, filled with the heat of the sun and the anger building in Chronos. He stared at the woman, wondering what she would do with his magic clock, but he was afraid to utter the words. So many possibilities were frightening. The most terrifying was his magic clock would be in the hands of someone he didn't trust. She had her own agenda which sometimes ran contrary to his plans.

Letting out a cynical laugh, she told him, "Don't look at me so hard, Chronos. I want it for a good reason. You can show me how to call back my species that are gone from the earth. It's all I want. To bring back my extinct friends. That's not too much to ask of you, is it?"

"Yes." He took a step back. "Yes, it's too much to ask. No, I won't let you have it."

Terra's lower lip stuck out, and her eyes moistened. "But Chronos, they're my babies! Just like that little girl is your grandbaby, those species are my babies. Please help me bring them back."

Father Time shook his head. "I can't. Once some things are gone, they're gone forever. Even the clock can't bring everyone—or everything—back from the dead. The clock is mine. I will not give it away." He turned away from her and faded from sight.

Mother Nature's eyes narrowed. She twirled so quickly the lunar dust turned into a whirlwind as she left the moon to go back to Earth. On the nearby planet, a low-pressure system began to form in the middle of an ocean.

A group of atmospheric scientists at the National Weather Service huddled around the spiral radar image looping on the computer screen. No one moved. They were transfixed by the massive storm nearly covering the entire Gulf of Mexico. The superimposed outline of the United States coastline almost shivered in fear of where the storm would choose to come onshore. A blue line marked the atmospheric model's prediction of the storm path over the western coast of Florida.

"Looks bad," one man understated.

"Real bad," said another. Crossing his arms, he further declared, "If the models are right, the Louisiana and Alabama coasts will get hammered."

"More like sledge-hammered," said a woman. She adjusted her glasses as she leaned in closer.

The woman in front of the monitor asked, "Is it time to make a few calls? Early warnings will save more people."

A scientist in a white shirt with rolled up sleeves, a tie, and three pens in his pocket protector stood up and stretched backwards. "Not yet. Where does the European model say it will come onshore?"

Clicking and mousing conjured up a red line that curved and widened its way in another direction from the blue line.

"Says the storm will make landfall on the west coast of Florida."

Moaning, groaning, a quiet smattering of cursing floated above the computer screen. "Might as well alert the whole Gulf Coast. Helene could land anywhere."

One voice of laughter lifted above the continued moaning. "Fitting name for a hurricane that size. It's my great-aunt's name. She left a lot of destruction in her wake too."

"This isn't funny."

"I know. Just ironic."

A female scientist changed the subject. "Where did this storm come from? It's not followed the typical storm track. It boiled up from nowhere. If this is what we have in store with global warming, we're in deep kimchi."

"It's an anomaly. No one knows what caused it for sure, so we need to gather data and study it."

The pocket-protector supervisor decided the immediate agenda. "Gather the data but analyze it later. Watch it closely until Helene makes up her mind where she's going. It's up to us to broadcast a warning about its path, potential destructive force and save as many people as we can."

One man snorted. "People don't listen anymore. They're more concerned about their property than their safety."

Kiboshing the discussion, the supervisor settled the matter. "Let's wait six more hours and see if the models come together. We may know its projected path better so we can make the right call. Valerie, call the Coast Guard again and let them know what's going on out there in the gulf. Helene is building and will only get worse. They'll have their hands full if any shrimping boats are out on those waters." He signaled for his crew to get back to work and rerun the models as he left. The group broke up, returning to their individual computers.

Six hours later, the same group gathered around a computer screen again. The European and American models were closer together, although not completely aligned. Their best guess was Helene was headed for the upper and west coasts of Florida. The Category 5 storm would decimate the Florida and Georgia coastlines and far inland. Chances were high that flooding in the southeastern U.S. would set records.

The supervisor stood rubbing his mustache and goatee as they all stared at the spiral-filled monitor screen. His crew's eyes were on him, waiting for a signal.

Impatient to wait longer, a woman asked, "Time to make the calls?"

Nodding, the supervisor stated in an edgy voice, "Light up the phones, team."

Chapter 2

Essie

Essie Bunny's cell phone vibrated in the pocket of her slacks as she folded the last of the laundry. Pulling it out and giving it a glance, she shoved it back into her pocket. Her sister, Sharon Claus, was calling. Again. No doubt to bug her about returning to the cottage for one last visit with their dead mother.

Her pocket tickled her leg as the phone vibrated. "Quit calling me," she shouted at the still ringing phone. With a huff, she took it out of her pocket and dropped it onto a pile of unfolded, clean laundry. As she moved the wet clothes to the dryer, another cheerful tune came from her cell phone, signaling her other sister, Hannah Horseman, was trying to reach her. Throwing a folded towel on top of the unfolded laundry slightly muffled the sound. Her nerves were in no shape to listen to either sister's call to whine about meeting in Florida. Too many other things needed her attention.

She knew what they wanted. They wanted to see their mother. Her two sisters had each set the magical clock to three o'clock, and their mother emerged from the grandfather clock both times. Hers was the last opportunity to call their mother back. Even thinking about it made her insides hurt. She wasn't ready to embrace her mother for the last time.

A sense of power warmed her bones. The three sisters had mutually agreed not to visit the cottage until they could be there with their families for the last visit. With school starting for her thirteen children in a few days, this was not a good time for a vacation to Florida. Until a time came that worked out for her family, there'd be no visit to her mother's cottage. And that might be a long time. Until then, she'd hold onto the anticipation of seeing her mother one more time.

Her oldest children, Pete and Marcia, were leaving for the university in a few days. The next oldest twins, Sylvie and Clara, had their exams coming up that would place them on the vocational or academia educational track. There was no time for a trip to Florida, no matter how fast Santa's sleigh could get them there and back. The trip would disrupt the focus needed for these important life-steps.

"Mom." Essie looked up from folding clothes as Sadie came in.

Her daughter slumped on the floor by the warm dryer as it tossed the wet clothes around. Her chin quivered as she lay prone on the floor. The static electricity in her hair made it stand on end, almost eliciting laughter from Essie, but her daughter's distraught face brought control over the impulse.

With a snap of a tee shirt, Essie looked away and sighed, "Something wrong?" She smoothed the shirt before folding it neatly.

"I don't want Marcia and Pete to leave."

Deep, deep down, neither did she, but it was time for them to fly. She and Easter didn't raise their children to live at home all their lives. They'd been taught how to take care of themselves and would do well without them. As a bonus, her budget would go a little farther by saving money on food, plus the laundry pile wouldn't be quite as high. Essie was determined to keep focused on the advantages and focus less on how much she'd miss having them around.

With another snap, she lay another tee shirt flat to smooth the last wrinkles out of it. "It'll be fine. You'll get used to it."

Another voice charged in from the hallway. "Mom, I can't find my black socks." Pete stuck his head in the laundry room door. "You seen them? Ah!" He grabbed a pair of socks from the mountain of folded laundry and started to leave.

"Wait a minute!" Essie grabbed his arm. "As long as you're here, take your clothes please, and take your brothers' clothes with you."

"My arms aren't that big!"

"Try anyway."

A moan, a groan, and wide-stretched arms raked up a pile of folded clothes sitting on the table. Her son bound for the university plodded off like he was carrying a giant piece of lead, muttering something about being free from chores in college. Dragging his feet because he had to do something for his brothers. Going off to school and discovering the duties of living away from home would be good for him.

"If they get messed up, you'll fold them again!" she yelled after him.

Another bonus of them leaving the house—two less people to complain.

Her husband, Easter, came in the laundry room and stared at his daughter lying on the floor. "What's wrong with her?"

Folding the last shirt, Essie replied, "She's sad because she'll be lonely when Marcia and Pete leave for college."

"But there'll still be thirteen of us here. How can she be lonely in that crowd?"

Sadie shot up. "You guys don't understand how I feel! You don't understand anything!" Her bottom lip came out as she crossed her arms.

Picking up the neatly folded stack of laundry, Essie handed it to Sadie. "Sorry, hon, we try to understand, but since we don't, take these to your room and put them up."

The pouty lip was sucked in as her eyes narrowed. She snatched the clothes and stomped off, grumbling about clueless parents.

Her mother and father stared after her until she turned a corner and disappeared. Essie looked at Easter who looked at her, waiting to see who would break first. When Easter got a crooked smile on his face, Essie released her long-held-back eye roll. Enveloping her in his arms, Easter whispered, "She's fifteen and a drama queen. She'll get over it."

Essie gave him a squeeze. "When?" She pushed him away and turned back to the laundry. "Since you don't have anything to do, help me get this distributed to the right rooms. And if you utter one word of complaint, I'm not cooking."

Laughing, Easter picked up one of the baskets filled to the rim. His chocolate egg factory was being cleaned before starting production for the upcoming Easter egg season. It was the only time he had a little reprieve from working daily in his factory.

Together they went along the long hallway of their underground house. Going into bedrooms in opposite directions, moans of protest preceded them out the door as they emerged with fewer clothes in their baskets. Essie paused as she yelled, "Either put your clothes up or clean the bathroom. Your choice." Instant quiet descended over the household.

Easter's eyes were wide as they continued down the hallway. "You seem a bit tense."

Rubbing her forehead, she replied. "Too many people asking me to do something for them. I'm tired of it. It's like being slowly pushed toward the edge of insanity."

"You should take a little time for yourself. "Have you talked to your sisters lately? They might meet you at the cottage—"

"No!"

Easter's big feet had stepped on the only nerve left for her. "My sisters are part of the problem. The kids are another part. I'm warning you, don't become part of the problem." She heard a snarl and she wondered what child had brought a dog home. She looked around before realizing the sound had come from her. The edge was creeping closer.

Easter's body tensed beside her as his fingers did a jig on the edge of the basket. "I may know why they're trying to call you. I saw a snippet of weather news talking about a big hurricane in the Gulf of Mexico heading toward Florida. They may be afraid for the cottage."

Essie turned into the large bedroom their youngest three sons shared. Toy trucks were scattered across the floor like land mines, and boyish laughter drifted out from under the bed. Not in the mood to deal with it, she dropped the laundry basket on the floor. "Put your clothes away. Take the basket back to the laundry room when you're done. And clean this mess up! I'll be checking on you later." Silence accompanied her exit.

With one cocked eyebrow, Easter stared at her. Though his flexible nose hung on his face like a drip down the side of a candle, his loving heart had captured hers, and they'd been happy together for 21 years. Just not at this particular moment. Right now, he was annoying her.

"I didn't know that. I haven't talked to either one in quite a while. Sharon aggravates me constantly about going back there. She calls me several times a day, but lately, I've been ignoring her calls." She pulled the phone from her pocket and looked at the voice mail icon with the number eight on it. "Looks like she left me another message."

"You need to talk to her. It might be important. It's rude of you not to answer."

Tired of the conversation, she turned her back. "And you need to leave me alone."

Silently they walked across the hall to the girls' empty bedroom. They'd either heard their brothers being yelled at and fled, or they were hiding. Not caring either way, Essie took clothes from his basket and put them on their beds.

Finished with the chore, she made her way to their bedroom. "I don't want to talk to my sisters because all they do is pressure me about gathering the family and going to Mother's cottage. They want to call her back for her last visit. I've told and told them, it's not a good time. What with Pete and Marcia headed off to the university, and Sylvie and Clara studying for their exams, and the other children going back to school next week, we can't get away right now." She turned away from him and opened their closet door.

As she took the last of the clothes from his basket, she glanced at Easter.

Tears moistened his eyes. He set the basket on the floor and got out his handkerchief to wipe his eyes. "Do you know how lucky you are to have your sisters? To have one more day with your mother? I'd give anything to see my mother once more…"

His voice gave way to sadness right before his hand went to his chin to stop its quivering. "Talk to your sisters long enough to set a date. How about next summer when everyone is out of school? I bet Sharon won't call anymore if you give her a date. Or better yet, use that talisman around your neck and snap in to see her. Take an hour or two and visit your sisters. You'll probably feel better after you do."

The stack of clothes in her arms gave off a mild flowery scent, triggering memories. Her mother loved flowers and always planted different varieties around the cottage. Their fragrance filled the yard and their cottage almost year-round. Essie missed her childhood days. "Maybe you're right."

Her husband tilted his head to the side. "Aren't I always?"

Essie's heart swelled with love for her man. With her arms full of folded clothes, she gave him a soft kiss before putting them away. Having everything put away softened her mood a little.

He put his arm around her as they walked back to the laundry room with the empty basket. Once there, he embraced her for a better kiss which was interrupted by a bang and a scream from the hallway. Rising voices throwing blame around like a hot potato drifted to the couple.

Essie heaved a sigh. "It never ends. Time to referee."

"No," Easter said as he let her go. "Let me." As he moved into the hallway, his voice boomed around the house, "The next person who yells at a sibling, touches a sibling, or even looks at a sibling will be scrubbing the floor in the factory."

Silence spread like a mudslide down the hallway.

He turned, spreading his arms wide in expectation of praise. "You're welcome. Get your phone and call your sister, or I'll have you cleaning the floors." Giving her a smile and a wink, he left her alone with her cell phone and her empty laundry basket.

Easter's threat was real. He was a stickler about keeping his factory spotless and in top sanitary shape. The floor seemed like ten acres of tile, and manually mopping it was a physically hard, back-tweaking job. Several times she'd felt the aches in her shoulders and the rawness of her hands from pushing the big mop around and under the machines. Since

14

the children were older, the chore was used to keep them in line, although their father helped them quite a bit. Pete and Sylvia spent a day there after they'd played soccer in the house and broke a light fixture. Thomas spent two days cleaning after skipping school to go to town with friends. Their stories about the horror of scrubbing equipment and sweeping up put the fear in the other children. But mischief always finds children and in time, the younger ones would serve their sentences mopping the factory floor.

Essie's cell phone vibrated in her pocket again. Her mind flashed a vision of Sharon pacing in her home at the North Pole, a paper bag over her face. Anxiety often visited Sharon, making her hyperventilate. She usually had a paper bag close by to help slow her oxygen intake. Despite her display of courage as she faced the ghosts squatting in their mother's cottage three years ago, her anxiety issues returned and made her seem weak.

The phone vibrated again, bringing Essie's attention back from where it had wandered. A vision of mopping dirty tile floors replaced the one of Sharon. The phone again beckoned her to answer. Pulling the phone from her pocket, her sister Hannah's phone number shone at her. Taking a deep breath, she steeled herself and put a fake smile in her vocal cords. She pushed the Accept button. "Hannah! How nice to hear from you! It's been a long time."

"Essie, there's a hurricane headed for Mother's cottage."

Hannah's tone wiped the phony smile out of Essie's voice. No greeting? No how are you? No pleasantness in her voice? The door on Hannah's cordiality slammed shut. She opened her mouth to speak but was cut off.

"It's a big one," Hannah told her. "Likely to cause all kinds of damage. Can you and Easter go take care of the cottage to minimize the storm's effects? Nothing big. Just board up the windows and sandbag the doors."

Nothing big? By whose definition? There was nothing to consider. Essie's calendar of upcoming events was full. "I can't go. Why can't you and Headless go?" Her voice matched the resentment Hannah's voice portrayed.

A light drumming sound came through, carrying with it a long, drawn-out sensation of impatience. "Why do we have to do everything?" Hannah's voice held unfiltered annoyance.

The logic seemed perfectly clear to Essie. "Because you're the closest. And besides, you don't do everything! The cottage sits there. Empty. That hardly requires your attention."

"I pay the bills," Hannah barked, her annoyance tone having moved to one of anger. "I snap there to make sure it's not disturbed or vandalized. I make sure the taxes are paid on time. I. Do. Everything."

Answers, retorts, and opinions flew through Essie's mind as she pulled out her father's necklace from her shirt. Twirling it in her hand reflected her mind's state. Nothing came to mind to refute Hannah's claim. She hadn't given her mother's cottage a thought since coming home three years ago. Her children kept her too busy to think about anyplace other than her own home. Only Sharon's occasional nagging calls reminded her of other responsibilities extended to the other side of the world.

Storm or no storm, she couldn't get away until the school year settled in a routine. Getting thirteen children ready for school and the university was a full-time job that included a lot of overtime. "Did you ask Sharon if she and Santa could go?"

"Have you talked to her lately?"

"No. It's been several weeks. She called me so many times, nagging and nagging about calling Mother back, I finally quit answering her calls. I can't do it now for the same reason I can't go board up the cottage. We have kids getting ready to go off to college, other kids with placement tests coming up—"

"We all have problems. My boys are in school too and have lots of afterschool activities. I'm a taxi driver more than a mother anymore."

Scrunching up her face, Essie pinched the bridge of her nose. "All the more reason to get Sharon and Santa and some of their elves to do it. They don't have anyone going to school so they should have time. It's not Christmas yet." Her foot started tapping uncontrollably. "And they have a work force neither of us do."

"Sharon's in no shape to help with it."

"Is she sick?"

An aggravated humming came through the broadband. "Not physically. You don't know about her dream?"

"No."

"Want to hear about it?"

The hallway seemed quiet. Easter must have successfully engaged the children. Or had them scrubbing the factory floor. A rare quiet time for herself. Spending time on the phone with Hannah wasn't her idea of the best use of the quiet, but there was no avoiding it. Going into the den, she nestled into a comfortable chair and invited the conversation.

Hannah told her on a recent night, Sharon had dreamt someone had died and the sisters couldn't call their mother back. Since Essie was the only one who hadn't called her, Sharon assumed Essie was the one who died in her dream. It seemed so real she'd been overwhelmed by the anxiety of losing a sister.

Going on, Hannah explained Santa had tried to call to Essie and get her to come to the North Pole to comfort Sharon. Having no success with that, he'd called Hannah asking for help in persuading Essie to make the trip to call their mother back one last time.

Essie sat unmoving in the chair. Sharon had never had premonitions before. ESP was a figment of people's imagination. Nobody knew when they would die. Maybe the dream wasn't specifically about her. Maybe Hannah would die. The thought sent a shudder through Essie, leaving her trembling like a leaf on an aspen tree.

She shook her head. It was a bad dream. Why would Sharon give credence to it? Her anxiety. It made her imagination run wild with the worst-case scenarios imaginable. No doubt it had run away with her again. She needed to realize her dream was only a dream. Wasn't it?

A few butterflies circled in her stomach. "Why didn't she tell me?"

"She tried. Santa tried. But you didn't answer your phone. Plus, how do you call your sister and say, 'You're going to die so let's go call Mother back before you do.' Sounds a little calloused and not something someone as nice as Sharon would say."

Squeamishness embraced Essie and made her fidget in her seat. Her schedule had no time for death. She was only in her mid-forties. That was too young to die. Her mother had lived to an old age and her father was immortal so she had longevity genes inside. She couldn't die young. What would her family do without her? No, not possible.

"That's silly. I'm not going to die. At least not yet. My family needs me. It was only a dream, right?" As the words were uttered, a tremor shook her and her voice.

Hannah took longer to answer than expected. "Of course," she said half-heartedly. "But call Sharon about it. It may set her mind at ease. Let's get back to why I called. Someone needs to go tonight to board the cottage up before the hurricane hits. The weather guys say it's a big one with a twelve-foot storm surge. I think the cottage will be damaged, but we don't know to what extent."

"And the clock?"

Silence. Hannah cleared her throat. "Not sure. It's a magical clock, but I'm not sure it will withstand a Class 5 hurricane."

"We should talk to Father."

"Call for him while you're boarding up the cottage. He may come, but it seems he's always busy so it's takes a while. There's no time to wait for him to answer." She sighed, releasing an annoyed sound with it. "This problem is ours. Look, if you two go, I'll get Headless to come help. With the four of us, it shouldn't take long. Just four or six hours. Surely you can spare that much time."

Essie rubbed her face with her free hand. She clenched her teeth to keep from screaming in frustration. Fine. She and Easter could go board up the cottage even though they didn't have time and didn't want to. Her mother's cottage had been there for years, through other hurricanes and storms, and yet it stood. Why would this one be any different?

She didn't want to spend the time and had no inclination to go, but she had little motivation to argue. "I can spare a couple of hours, but that's it. If it can't be done in that amount of time, I can't go. I don't think it's necessary. Father would never let anything happen to the clock. It'll be fine."

"I don't think enthusiasm is measured by negative numbers, but I think you've done it." Hannah let out a lament of frustration. "Check the weather maps if you don't believe me. This is developing into a huge storm! We have to get the plywood from the store, nail it up, and seal the windows and doors from the storm surge."

"And the clock!" Essie blurted out. "Something must be done to protect the clock."

A loud growl came through the line. Hostility tainted Hannah's voice. "We need strong backs to move it to higher ground. We need Headless and Easter for a job that big. We can't possibly do it in a couple of hours. It'll take much longer!"

Essie's phone was almost hot from her sister's anger surging through the connection. The conversation was tiring. If it didn't cost so much to replace the phone, she'd throw it against the wall, the modern form of hanging up on an unwanted caller. The End button called to her. One push and she'd be away from the hounding.

"Come on, Essie, fair is fair. We'll meet you there tomorrow morning. Our time."

A huge sigh emanated from Essie. "I'll try, but don't count on us. We're just too busy." Satisfied the call was over, she hit the End button so hard her fingertip throbbed for a few seconds. She stuck it in her mouth and sucked the hurt away.

Chapter 3

Sharon

Outside the stone house at the North Pole, an early blizzard swirled and stacked snowflakes into deep piles. Inside, a roaring fire in the large hearth added warmth to Santa's office where he sat staring at his computer screen. The latest naughty-nice list had been posted.

In the corner of Santa's office, Sharon Claus sat in a comfortable chair by her reading lamp, a book in her lap. She thumbed the clock-shaped pendant on the necklace her father had given her. She wore it constantly.

The book didn't interest her so she wasn't actually reading—just pretending to so Santa didn't ask too many questions.

Her mind couldn't rid itself of the horrible dream she'd had the week before. Her heart felt like it was in one of the vises in Santa's workshop. Her body couldn't rid itself of the tension gripping her because her calls to Essie went unanswered. Panic had almost paralyzed her since the dream. It took every ounce of mental strength to get out of bed in the mornings and go about her day. She feared never seeing her mother again, but more than that, she feared losing her sister. Ever since she and her sisters made up and were speaking to each other again, she didn't know what she'd do if she lost one. She valued their renewed relationships more than either sister knew. So much so, the potential loss of it was choking the life out of her.

Picking up her cell phone, Essie's name appeared at the top recent-calls list. Her finger hovered over the call button.

She wanted to call again, but it would likely lead to the same disappointment she'd experienced the last time she allowed her finger to push the button. Was she ready to face rejection again? She quickly put the phone down and picked up her book.

"You want me to try calling her?" Santa was turned in his chair, staring at her over the wire-rimmed glasses low on his nose.

Sharon leaned her head back against her chair and stared at the ceiling. Above her, the slow-moving ceiling fan turned in a slow circle, much like her arguments with herself. Never going anywhere, just turning. Turning. She shut her eyes. "No. She probably won't answer your call either."

He rose to come to her, pulling up a tall stool and sitting near her. Folding his glasses and putting them in his large pocket, he said, "Then snap over to see her. She doesn't understand your situation. Seeing her face-to-face might persuade her to go to Florida." He held up his hand before she could rebut what he said. "It doesn't matter if you three decided to go only when the families could. It's not going to work out that way. You have to face it. Life has become too complicated to coordinate such a big group. Change your plans to fit the changed situation."

She stared at the face of her husband. The twinkle in his eye dimmed when he worried about her, and a new wrinkle crossed his forehead. Her worries were taking a toll on him. She shook her head. "I wanted Sam to visit with Mother one last time."

"I know," he said as he took her hands. "But that proves my point. He started his new job in London and can't come for a while. By then, he might have different priorities." Raising her hands to his lips, he kissed them softly. "Life changes plans. Besides, he got to see her twice. That's two times more than anyone else gets after a loved one passes."

Pulling her hands from his, she slammed the book shut. A tissue was pulled from the sleeve of her sweater and used to dab her eyes as she looked up at the fan again. "You're right, but how do I persuade the other two. They want their kids to see her." She let out a sigh of resignation. "But with Essie's kids going off to school and Hannah's boys in several sports, there's never going to be a time for us to get together. Except maybe for a funeral. People make time for those." Her eyes blurred, and she quickly shut them to keep more tears back. Her tissue was becoming too damp. "When my dream comes true, they'll suddenly have time."

Santa was quickly at her side, leaning against the arm of the chair with his arms around her. "I'm telling you, Sharon, it was only a bad dream. It wasn't a premonition. You've never been psychic, and I doubt you're developing the talent now. Everybody has bad dreams every now and again, but that's all they are. Dreams."

She waved him off. Her head knew he was right, but her heart was racked with the image of her dream. Darkness and a roaring surrounded a figure lying on the floor of the cottage. It was someone she knew. Someone who was dear to her. Blood flowed from the person's head. The person was alone and helpless, and no one came to their aid. As the scene faded, her mother's voice said, "I can't come back."

Darkness seemed to press in on Sharon. Her chest was tight as she gasped for air. The room moved like it was floating on water, rocking back and forth.

Santa pushed a paper bag over her face. "Slow your breathing, honey."

Clutching the bag, she held it over her mouth and nose.

He leaned closer. "Watch me. Breath with me." He slowly took in a breath and held it a few seconds before releasing it in a long exhale. "It's panic. It's fear overwhelming your brain when it shouldn't be." He repeated the breathing technique.

Following his lead, Sharon breathed along with him, slowing her gasping to a crawl. Her twirling mind slowed as she breathed into the bag. The room settled and remained stationary. The rumpling bag measured her breaths as she gradually returned to her normal self, breathing calmly and in more control.

She lowered the bag into her lap. "That was a bad one."

Even though the worry wrinkle on Santa's forehead was still there, his eyes were more relaxed as he took the crumpled bag from her. "I'm glad you made your way through it. Remember what the doctor said. Acknowledge it as a panic attack. You'll feel bad for a little bit, but it will pass, and you'll be yourself again."

Nodding, she took his face in her hands and planted a kiss on his rosy cheek. "You always know how to make me feel better."

He let out a soft ho-ho-ho as he returned to his chair. "It's been a while since you had therapy. You should think about returning to the kitchen. I think the workshop is running low on cookies."

Sharon loved cooking and baking. The joy of blending raw ingredients into delicious foods and smelling the aroma of baking cinnamon, chocolate, and vanilla was like an antidepressant for her. The anticipation of spending time in her kitchen forced a smile to break out on her face. "We can't run out of snacks so I better get busy. I'll take stock of what ingredients I have and send Elwin out for more supplies if I need them."

"He'll enjoy getting out. He hasn't gone into town for a long time. His wife will be happy he has someplace to go." He put his reading glasses back on his nose and went back to his computer.

A huge weight fell off her as she rose from her chair. With something other than her fears to think about, her mind felt more at ease. Her fingers were counting off what she'd need to get started as she hurried to the kitchen for therapy.

Soon, she had Elwin on his way to the store for more supplies. The work sleigh would get him above the weather and to Nome in no time. Using what ingredients she had, she stirred up several bowls of cookie dough before anyone else joined her.

Sharon's best friend, Martha Elf, lifted a pan of cookies from the oven. "It's nice to have you back in the kitchen, Sharon. I missed you this past week."

Sharon had an arm around a large bowl as she pushed the spoon through the peanut-butter cookie batter. Her many years of manually stirring up batches of cookies left her with strong arms. No one else at Santa's house or in his workshop could stir a bowl of cookie dough like she could.

"I'm sorry about leaving everything to you." She put the bowl aside so she could hug her friend. "My anxiety got the best of me. I'm sorry."

Martha's short stature was no measure of her heart. She held on tight around Sharon's waist. "We all have our crosses to bear. I wish I could help you carry yours, but I can't." Pulling away, she ran a finger across the bottom of her eye. "My girls helped me and enjoyed it. They need to learn how to cook. Someday they may replace me in the kitchen."

A shudder went through Sharon. She went back to her bowl of dough and stirred with a vigor fueled by inner turmoil. Since her dream, the death theme seemed to pop up in the most unexpected places. Her panic attack made her think she was dying. Santa's oldest reindeer had to be put down a few days ago. Martha was talking about her girls taking her place after she was gone. Anticipatory grief was sucking the cheerfulness out of her home. With the strength of a weightlifter, she stirred the cookie dough like it was cake batter.

"There's not going to be anything left of those cookies if you don't lighten up."

A glance at Martha caused guilt to prick Sharon when she realized she was scaring her friend with her attack on the baking ingredients. She let go of the bowl with the overmixed dough.

"I guess those are stirred enough." Sharon wiped her hands on the bottom of her apron.

Martha blinked her wide eyes and nodded.

"Excuse me." Santa peeked around the corner into the kitchen. "Martha, could you finish these cookies? I need to talk to Sharon."

"Of course, Mr. Claus. That's a good idea." Martha took the bowl to a shorter table where several cookie sheets lay ready to be filled.

Wiping her hands on a dishtowel, Sharon leaned against Santa who led her back into his office. He motioned for her to sit in his desk chair, and she obeyed.

The monitor showed a map of the United States, with shifting white clouds across the map. Her preoccupied brain couldn't comprehend what she was looking at until Santa provided the interpretation.

"See this spot here?" His finger pointed to a spiraling group of clouds. "This is a hurricane. It's headed for Florida." He paused.

"For Florida?" her voice squeaked.

He swiveled the chair so she faced him. "I hate to add this burden to your anxiety-filled load, but it's headed for your mother's cottage. And they say it's a bad one."

An image of the cottage on the Florida beach flashed across her mind's eye. The sunny beach, the waves licking at the sand, the sea grass waving in the breeze. Other hurricanes had gone through there and yet the scene had remained pretty much the same. The cottage still stood, sheltering the clock inside, safe and dry.

She shook her head. "Father wouldn't let anything happen to the cottage, especially with the clock there. There's no need to worry."

Santa's head dropped to his chest right before he heaved a sigh. He flexed his fingers a few times before speaking. "The meteorologists are saying this is an unusual storm. It seemingly came out of nowhere and grew in strength quickly. I think—mind you, this is my opinion— something's different about this storm. I think you and your sisters need to go batten down the hatches and make sure the clock stays high and dry."

"But dear, you know we agreed not to visit the cottage unless we go together. And we also agreed not to go unless our whole families could go. I can't break my word. I'm sure our father will protect the clock from being damaged, and he'll save the cottage too." She patted his rosy cheek. "I appreciate your concern, but you shouldn't worry about it."

He stared at her. "You're not hearing me. This storm, it's a beast. And it seems to be drawing a bead on the cottage. On the news sites, they show people nailing plywood over the windows and filling sandbags. Forget the agreement and do what it takes to save the cottage. Otherwise, you might not see your mother again, and not because Essie didn't call her, not because your dream came true, but because a storm destroyed the cottage because you and your sisters did nothing to save it."

Santa's eyes held no twinkle, only concern wrapped in fear. Her heart shifted into a higher gear. Any threat to the enchanted clock was—was unthinkable. It had stood in the cottage all her life. Nothing came close to harming it before. Why now? A shudder ran through her.

"I need to talk to Essie and Hannah."

"Good idea, sweetheart. But better yet, get them both to snap up here. You can talk face-to-face and decide how to handle the situation. Make it a fun occasion. Serve them lunch or have a tea party." He took a sniff of the air. "I smell peanut butter cookies baking. You already have the treats to serve."

Ignoring his invitation to do it his way, she replied, "They're busy as usual. You know Essie with all those kids—"

A rare eyeroll from Santa preceded his sigh. "Whatever. A group decision needs to be made, and that's hard to do via the phone." He leaned in closer. "Use your magical necklace to go see them. I'll tell Martha you had to rest for a while and not to disturb you. She can get her girls to help her with meals again."

Panic started building in Sharon, making her breathe too fast. Santa held out a wrinkled paper bag, but she pushed it away. "Maybe you're right. I should go see Hannah. If Essie could meet us there, it wouldn't take long to decide what to do. I could snap right back so fast that Martha would think I'd taken a nap. If Martha can manage lunch one more time, I'll make it up to her later."

"Good plan." Santa helped her out of the chair. "Take an overnight bag, in case it takes longer than expected. I'll cover for you. I'll invent some excuse. Come now, let's get this done before I have to go feed the reindeer."

Sharon's arm encircled his girth, and Santa wrapped her in his arms. Sheltered from her worries in his embrace, she never wanted to leave. She'd have stayed there all day, but he pushed her away, mumbling something about needing to get to work.

It didn't take her long to pack a bag. With a final look around, she took hold of the talisman around her neck.

"Pop my bubble, I'm in trouble, take me there on the double. Hannah's living room."

The familiar squeezing and spinning gripped Sharon for an instant before she found herself swaying and slightly dizzy in what she assumed was Hannah's living room. She'd expected to see something similar to the Addams family home in the movies. To her surprise, the room looked normal. Neat and well-decorated, the large room held dark leather furniture on top of hardwood floors. A stone fireplace across from the sofa gave the place a quaint and welcoming touch. A huge television hung above it like a giant black eye. A large archway opened into a spacious, modern kitchen with an eating bar. Her heart felt a little lighter knowing her strange younger sister was normal in some way.

A voice from behind her loudly whispered, "What are you doing here?"

Sharon turned around to see her brother-in-law, Headless Horseman, standing there in a white tee shirt and flannel lounge pants. Below the brace holding his head on his shoulders, the line along his neck showing where it used to be attached to his head was plainly visible. The place his head was severed held her eyes, and she couldn't look away. Her hand flew to her throat, and she took a step back.

The sound of boys stomping on the staircase cascaded around them. Headless grabbed Sharon's arm and her overnight bag and pushed her through the kitchen and into a laundry room. Shutting the door behind him, he spun around to face her. "What are you doing here?" he iterated.

His angry eyes sent waves of fear through her. Even Captain Fremont hadn't scared her as much. "I—I—well, I came to see about shutting the cottage up before the big storm. I should have called before coming here. I'm sorry. I'll go." She grabbed the necklace. "Pop my bubble—"

Headless took her hand away from the talisman, interrupting her chant. "Look, I'm sorry to be so brusque, but we can't let the boys see you. They'll ask a bunch of questions about how you got here." He listened at the door as the boys came into the kitchen.

"Where's breakfast?" one of them called out. "I thought Dad was making it."

"Eat cereal or make it yourself." Hannah's voice sounded like she was somewhere other than the kitchen. "Your dad is outside feeding the horses instead of you."

Cereal bowls clanked and spoons clattered with the unseen activities. Headless stood with his hands on his hips, tapping his foot while he and Sharon listened to the school-morning voices of Horace and Huntley as they ate their breakfast. The talk of homework, soccer practice, and friends drifted through the door.

Cheerful children's voices always delighted Sharon. Her nephews were well adjusted and happy, giving her more reason to love them, but the sounds weren't enough to lift her out of her deep pit of embarrassment. She wanted to snap away or melt into the ground.

Santa's idea to snap there was a disaster. Judging from his expression, Headless agreed with that assessment.

His hands moved in funny ways as his eyes and motions exposed the inner argument he was having with himself. Panic began to bubble up like a geyser about to explode. With no paper bag handy, she put her hands over her mouth and nose and tried to calm down.

As if by magic, Headless quit his bouncing around and pulled out a stool for her to sit on. His head bobbled on its cradle as he helped her settle onto it. After he steadied it, he leaned over and whispered, "I'm sorry. I don't mean to make you nervous."

Shaking her head, Sharon answered as softly as she could, "No, I'm the one who's sorry. I'm an idiot for not calling first. I'll go home." Taking her talisman again, she prepared to recite the verse.

Again, he pulled her hands away from the talisman as he raised his eyebrows. "It's not that we don't want you here. The problem is knowing how to explain your presence. They'd think Santa brought you and would want to see the reindeer. My boys can't know about the talisman Mrs. Hagg gave you to transport anywhere you like. They'd want one, and it would be impossible to keep them home."

Regret filled her. "You're right of course. I didn't think about the boys. I'm sorry." She grabbed the necklace again. "I shouldn't have come."

For the third time, Headless took her hand away from the cord. "No, I'm sorry for being a jerk about it." A crooked smile moved his face. "I'm glad you came. Hannah's been desperate to get you and Essie here so the three of you can decide what to do with the cottage before the storm hits. If Essie knows you're here, maybe she'll come too."

Hearing the words lowered her panic level slightly. Her abrupt appearance might turn out to be acceptable and maybe even the best thing to have done. She lowered her shaking hands and held her breath. Sometimes that controlled her hyperventilating, but to be safe, she'd dig a paper bag out of her overnight case as soon as she could.

The noises in the kitchen died down as Headless nodded while talking to himself. "This might work out yet. Hannah needs to know you're here." Looking at Sharon again, he put his finger over his lips. "Stay in here and be quiet," he whispered. "The boys will be leaving for school soon."

"Yes, of course." She put her finger over her lips to affirm his instructions.

Headless took her by the shoulders. "By the way, nice to see you again, Sharon." He gave her a giant grin before leaving her in the laundry room.

Sharon looked around. The room smelled of horses, manure, and hay. Through another door, dusty work boots were neatly lined up against the wall. Coats hung from hooks above them. Through the window in the backdoor, she saw a path worn through the back yard leading to a barn where several dark horses flicked their tails and ate from a feed trough.

She softly closed the door between the mudroom and the laundry room, hoping the scent making her nose wrinkle would be lessened. She leaned against the washer as she waited to see what would happen next.

Hannah's voice drifted through the door, telling her boys to hurry up or they'd be late. The door to the laundry room swung open, making Sharon jump and nearly fall off the stool. With a sharp look and a frown, she grabbed two backpacks from a hook on the wall and left the room with a slam of the door.

Sharon buried her face in her hands. Headless might not mind her being there, but Hannah did. She'd felt the zap Hannah's look shot at her. She shouldn't have come. Taking the cord of the talisman in her hand, she paused, the words on her lips. It would be naughty of her to disappear without an explanation. If Hannah was mad she was here, she'd be madder if she left. What a mess she created for herself! What seemed like a good idea an hour ago had become a giant mistake. Hannah wasn't happy with her, and Headless was too nice of a person to tell her he felt the same as his wife. Plus, she was hiding from her nephews instead of smothering them in hugs and kisses.

Loud goodbyes and the sound of a slamming door signaled the boys had left for school. Sharon wondered if she should go to the living room or escape while she had a chance or wait until summoned. She opted for the latter.

Chapter 4

Hannah

Watching her boys climb into Huntley's car and head to school freed Hannah Horseman from her charade of courtesy. When Headless told her Sharon had snapped into the middle of their morning routine, she was livid. Cell phones made it easier than ever to make a courtesy call before a visit. She should have asked if it was a good time to come. Waiting half an hour would have worked so much better.

To snap in, especially when her boys might have been present, was the ultimate in rudeness. If her boys found out about talismans that allowed instant transportation over great distances, it would be a disaster. She'd tell them about it someday, but she'd pick the time and place and have Mrs. Hagg's blessing to do so. She'd given her word to her friend to keep them secret, and she would keep her promise. Otherwise, Mrs. Hagg might take back her gift.

Her talisman was more than a way to see her sisters or a method for checking on the cottage. Huntley was headed to college next semester, and it provided a good way to check on him. Headless said that was unnecessary, he was mature enough to be on his own. Her head agreed with him, but her mother's heart said no. He was still her baby, and she needed assurances he was fine. She could snap there and see him without being noticed by Headless or Huntley.

Her son's car turned onto the road at the end of their long driveway. Shutting the front door, she spun around. Now to deal with Sharon. It was time to set her straight about talisman etiquette. Noises drew her into the kitchen. Headless was pouring three cups of coffee. His eyes moved to the laundry room door and back to her before he tapped his watch. With raised eyebrows, he took a cup of coffee and left.

The coffee warmed her throat and cooled her temper. Her calls to Essie to come help with the cottage had been a waste of time, but Sharon was here offering to help. The taller Essie would be more help holding up heavy sheets of plywood across a window while she nailed them in place. The short and chunky Sharon likely didn't have the same strength or stamina, but small help was better than none. They might have to settle with nailing the shutters closed, like Headless had suggested enough times she tired of it. That option would work better than leaving the windows and doors unprotected. Another swallow of coffee gave her the proper demeanor for dealing with Sharon.

A deep breath in front of the laundry room door cooled her anger to a slow simmer. A quick rub of her father's necklace around her neck reminded her to be kind. Swinging the door open provided a view of Sharon with both hands cupped over her nose and mouth. Hannah knew what the action meant. Sharon's anxiety was making her hyperventilate. The sight provoked sympathy for her sister and the condition she couldn't control.

The last of her anger melted like a popsicle on a hot summer day. "Hi, sis," Hannah said before enveloping her in a hug. "What a surprise!" Feeling no reciprocating arms around her, she stepped back.

Sharon wrung her hands as she looked away. "I'm sorry I snapped in like this. I'm sorry I didn't call. I'm sorry I almost let the cat out of the bag with our special talismans." She looked at Hannah with eyes like a dog caught chewing a slipper. "I was going to snap back home, but Headless wouldn't let me. If you want me to go—"

Hannah swiped the air with her hand, deflecting the words and the apology. "Don't worry about it. The boys still don't know so no harm done. I'm glad you came here." She bent a little so she could look into Sharon's eyes. "I'm not mad. Believe me?"

A smile cracked across Sharon's furrowed face as she nodded.

"How about a piece of toast and coffee?"

Sharon's eyes lit up. "Yes, please! I'm famished, and coffee will help me settle down. I missed my morning shot of caffeine."

Leading her into the kitchen, Hannah pushed a cup of coffee toward her before putting bread in the toaster. As she waited for it to brown, she gazed out the big window that looked out over a manicured lawn and the barn beyond. The faint sound of birds singing drifted through the glass. The sound of four pieces of toast popping out of the toaster drew her attention back to the problem at hand. She quickly buttered the toast and joined her sister at the eating bar. "You seem very—well, nervous. It's okay you're here. Or are you afraid of something else?"

Sharon rubbed the side of her coffee cup while she stared at the liquid inside. "The unknown." Picking up a piece of toast, she filled her mouth with a large bite.

The toast didn't make it to Hannah's mouth. She set it back on her plate as she stared at her sister. The unknown wasn't the kind of problem they could solve in a gab session. The root of it lay in Sharon's anxiety problem. Like an invisible sticker on the bottom of your foot, it constantly made its presence known and hindered everything.

It affected relationships too. Sometimes Hannah felt like she was walking on ice around Sharon, fearing what would set her off. Surely there was some medication that would help with it. Maybe she should see a doctor.

Quickly taking a sip of coffee before she voiced what she was thinking, she pushed the thought away. She'd mention it at a different time. Deep inside she felt a little guilty for being perturbed by Sharon instead of being more sympathetic.

Another sip of coffee and a bite of toast brought her thoughts around. Recalling the last time they saw each other, Hannah said, "You surprise me, Sharon."

Sharon's eyebrows shot up, and she pointed at herself while she chewed.

Hannah nodded. "Yes, you. You faced the ghosts in Mother's cottage without fear when most people would have run screaming. You faced Captain Fremont like he was the next-door neighbor you saw every day. You were so courageous. I thought perhaps you'd beaten your panic problem."

Sharon wiped her mouth with her napkin, then took a sip of coffee. Tapping her fingertips on the table, she replied, "Captain Fremont didn't scare me. He and his ghostly crew were like regular people, in some ways, although they were an ornery bunch."

They shared a laugh before Sharon continued. "Lately the panic inside me has been very bad. It started when I had the dream where Essie died. It felt so real. I haven't been able to function since then. Santa sent me here, hoping I could find some measure of peace talking to you."

With a heart sinking under an unwanted responsibility, she replied, "Why didn't you go see Essie? She's the one causing you stress. She's probably the one who can allay it."

Using her finger, Sharon pushed stray toast crumbs into a small pile. "She wouldn't answer my phone calls. With so many children around, I didn't dare take the chance of snapping in. The odds were against remaining unseen."

Hannah couldn't argue with that logic, but it didn't explain why she didn't call before visiting the Horseman house. Her having only two sons didn't relieve Sharon of good manners in calling before visiting. It also didn't explain why Sharon was at her house. Was she expected to be the counselor she needed?

As if reading her mind, Sharon continued. "Santa convinced me I might be of help to you. He checked the weather and saw a big storm headed toward the cottage. A hurricane. Did you know? He said we need to get Mother's cottage boarded up for the storm. I thought if I came, maybe Essie will come too and the three of us could get it ready for the storm." She stared at Hannah. "Why are you rolling your eyes?"

A cynical chuckle bolted out of Hannah. "I've tried and tried to get Essie to come, but she's 'too busy.' She's completely unconcerned about the hurricane and has no intention of helping."

Sharon pushed back her unfinished toast. "It might be best if she didn't come. My dream might come true. She might fall off a ladder or get hit by lightning or drown in the ocean. I wouldn't want her to take the chance."

"It was only a dream, Sharon." The words hovered in the air between them, waiting to be received by the one they were directed at.

Sharon's hand waved the words away like they were gnats around her face. "My head knows, but my heart doesn't. Please, let me go instead of her. If she went and something happened to her, I'd never be able to live with myself." The coffee in Sharon's cup shook slightly as she lifted it to her lips. A tightly twisted paper napkin lay in front of her. Taking several sips, her eyes stared at something unseen except by her.

Hannah watched her sister, unmoving, her mind lost somewhere inside. She'd seen her in the throes of a panic attack, but she didn't remember her being so paralyzed by fear. The dream had affected Sharon far more than she suspected. Her fear of the dream and the unknown future was real. To help her find her way back from the edge of her panic, Hannah had to get her to focus on something else.

Hannah redirected as she played with the handle of her coffee mug. "Since Essie's not going to help with the cottage, and you're willing to help, let's do it. We'll make a list of supplies we need to shut it up. We can buy plywood to nail over the windows and—"

"Won't happen," Headless said as he came into the kitchen. He had a turtleneck shirt on that hid his brace and neck. "I checked several of the hardware stores around Sarasota and nearby towns. There's no plywood for sale anywhere. The sand bagging sites are open, but no one is there to help fill them. Most people are evacuating or have already left. Unless you want to buy supplies here and snap over with them, you're out of luck."

Rubbing her temples as they pounded with the realization she'd waited too long to do something, her ire at Essie's procrastination flared, but also flared at her own idleness. Rather than doing what needed to be done with or without Essie, she'd waited for her, hoping she and Easter would help. She should have listened to Headless and asked Sharon and Santa before now. She'd discounted them because of—height. She'd been a fool. Because she didn't do enough, the loss would be to them all. Nature would evenly spread the consequences of their neglect.

She felt strong arms come across her shoulders. "Securing the shutters may be enough. I'll cancel my meeting today if you want me to go help."

Shaking her head without looking at him, she replied, "No, your appointment with the horse buyer was set a long time ago. Let's not get on his bad side by cancelling at the last minute. He loves our horses, and if we treat him right, he'll come back to buy more."

Stammering noises interrupted their conversation. "But—me—I'll help with the cottage," Sharon said as she pushed out her chair and stood. "Santa sent me here to see about it, and it's a good thing too. You need me." A smile lit up her face, and her mood seemed lighter in that instant. "I know I look like I do nothing but sit around and eat cookies all day, but I'm strong. Trust me, I can help board up the house." She flexed her arms as if she were a short, stocky bodybuilder. Her anxiety seemed to dissipate with her whimsical posing. Her laughter joined Hannah and Headless as they snickered at her.

There was nothing to do but make the best of whatever help they could get. Resigning herself to her circumstances, Hannah decided, "Nailing the shutters closed will have to do. If sandbags are available, we can pile them around the doors. I'm not sure what other preparations we can make."

Sharon's merrymaking stopped. "We have to protect the clock. Nothing must happen to it. We need it to call Mother and Father."

Tension tightened Hannah's shoulders as she stood. "It's too heavy to lift and there's no high ground to put it on. If we get enough sandbags, we'll put them around the clock. That would keep most of the water out." Even as she said the words, she also thought about the twelve-foot storm surge predicted. There weren't enough sandbags anywhere to keep that much water out. Rather than give Sharon another reason to panic, she kept it to herself.

Headless kneaded Hannah's shoulders. It didn't relieve the stress but accentuated how much tightness was there. She shrugged off his efforts to ease it. "I supposed we should take care of it while the boys are at school."

Pulling out his phone, he said, "According to the weather radar, the hurricane should make landfall tonight. Winds may reach 150 miles per hour or more. It's already starting to get bad there so you need to hurry. You'll have to do the best you can with what's at the house. Go in. Get it done. Get out. You don't want to get caught in the storm."

Ignoring her own rising panic, Hannah adjusted her voice to sound calm. "All we need to do is close the shutters and make sure the clock stays dry. The furniture and kitchen utensils are easily replaced. It shouldn't take long. Right, Sharon?"

"Right." Sharon's hands were trembling, but her face and her voice showed determination. "It's the reason why I came. I have a little experience with a hammer, although nailing brads on toys is different than nailing with big nails." A slight smile moved the corners of her mouth but didn't share it with her eyes. "Let's not tell Essie we're going."

"If it makes you feel better, we won't." Hannah downed the last of her coffee. "You and I can handle it. Let's gather two hammers and nails to affix the shutters closed. Headless, can you get those for us?"

Headless started toward the back door. "I'll get what I have and bag it up for easier carrying. You should take a raincoat or two or three or ten."

"I brought mine," Sharon said as she moved toward her suitcase.

Going to the coat closet, Hannah looked at her expensive raincoat. They were headed into a storm zone. Her good raincoat would keep her dry, but in hurricane conditions, her barnyard-chore raincoat would be adequate. An umbrella hung from the hanger bar. An umbrella in hurricane winds? Not unless she wanted a new umbrella. She slipped her sand shoes on. They were good in water.

Motioning to Sharon, Hannah said, "Let's go out to the barn and leave from there." As Sharon folded her raincoat over her arm, Hannah eyed her red sweat suit. "Are you okay in your heavy clothes, or do you want to change? I saw you brought a bag."

Sharon looked down and rubbed her hands along her sides. "These are my work clothes. I thought I was ready to go."

Looking at her tee shirt and yoga pants, Hannah decided it was better to say nothing than to point out to her northern-climes sister she was ill-dressed for Florida weather. The thick fabric might soak up water and make it heavy, impeding the work they needed to do. At least the anxiety and panic Sharon came with seemed to be more controlled. Opportunities for it to get out of control again would present themselves later.

With a faint thread of hope for success, Hannah waved her arm toward the back door. "Let's do this."

The two made their way to the barn where Headless had the necessary tools ready for them. Hannah fastened on the tool belt she'd used when she and Headless installed fencing around one of their pastures. The tools and nails were secured in the belt so they wouldn't fly off during their spinning transport.

With a snap, Hannah found herself in the middle of her mother's living room. She checked the carpenter's belt around her waist, relieved the hammer hadn't been lost during the vorticial transport. White sheets covered the furniture like a fresh snowfall. She and Headless had covered everything after a year and a half of no visits. Otherwise, the cottage remained as her mother left it. A little dust covered the surfaces, and the windows needed to be opened to let in fresh air. That chore would wait until after the hurricane, and after she got help from her sisters. Pulling the nails out of the shutters after the storm would take more than one person.

Sharon snapped in behind her. Sounds of wistful homecoming filled the room as she walked around. "I love this place. It's nice to see it again." She wandered into the kitchen. "I've missed you!" she pronounced to the walls. Hannah agreed.

Memories of her mother filled the cottage, carrying her back to her childhood. A few videotapes lay around the TV, a reminder of the happy childhood scenes recorded on them. A beach towel hung over the back of a chair, accidently left there after her family's last trip. Grabbing it, she rolled it around her arm and tossed it under the sofa to hide it. She hadn't told her sisters she and Headless had taken several day-long beach vacations at the cottage. She considered their visits as compensation for taking care of the place and its taxes.

Her sisters didn't know the cottage had become her secret getaway, made possible by Mrs. Hagg's incredible gift. Many middays found her swimming in the ocean or reading a book on the beach for a few hours. Her tanned skin should have been a giveaway of her activities, but no one seemed to notice, other than Headless who already knew.

Her mother's cottage was her peaceful place. Her frequent visits helped her keep a close eye on the cottage to make sure no unwanted visitors were there, natural or supernatural. If Sharon checked the closet in Hannah's old room, she'd find her beachwear there. A few protein bars, microwave popcorn, soda, and candy were tucked away in dark corners of the kitchen cabinets for times when the munchies hit.

The largest sheet draped the magical grandfather clock by the fireplace. Like a magnet, it drew the sisters close to it. Sharon pulled on the sheet until it slipped off. Mysterious secrets lay concealed inside the silent clock still showing nine-fifteen. Twice their mother had come out of the clock, giving them a day to visit and say the things they should have said when she was alive. The clock allowed each sister to call her back from the dead for one last visit. Only Essie's turn remained. Afterwards, their mother would be gone forever.

Sharon opened the face of the clock. "Let's set it to twelve and call Father. He could help us move the clock. He might have an idea how to protect it from a flood." She reached out to change the hands.

A strong gust of wind rattled the windows. Dread of being too late filled Hannah. The hurricane was due to hit the cottage after dark, but from the sound of the wind, it might make an early appearance. The already strong winds would get worse every minute until the monster storm came ashore. She should have boarded the place up earlier, with or without help from her sisters.

Hannah's hand shot out to hold back Sharon's hand before she put the hands in place. "No. He never comes right away, and what if he showed up during the worst part of the storm? The timing isn't good to call him now. We'll do the best we can to protect the clock. Father knows it's here and will watch out for it. It'll be fine, you'll see."

A loud bang made the women jump as if shocked by a bolt of electricity. When it happened again, Hannah knew for sure it came from outside. Looking out the front window, she saw the porch swing dancing to the rhythm of the strong gusty wind. "The porch swing is hitting the side of the house," she noted as the wind tossed it against the house again. "If it keeps hitting that hard, something's going to break."

Sharon's eyes widened as she bit her lip. Coming to look out the window, she replied, "Maybe we've come too late."

Hannah went toward the front door. "We're here so let's not waste time. We'll take the swing down first, then get the shutters secured before the wind kicks up anymore. After that, we'll come inside and set the clock to five. With time slowed in here, we'll have time to figure out what to do with the clock and get any other valuables secured before the storm."

Sharon went back to the clock's hands. "That's a good idea, but let's call Father now. He'll come while we're outside. He's always come when we needed him most, and we really need him now."

"No!" Hannah cried out as she rushed to the clock. The family's streak of stubbornness was raising its head at the most importune time. Standing in front of the silent timepiece, she stood firm. "There's no time! We have work to do!" Another bang against the wall accentuated the lack of time. She pushed the reluctant sister toward the front door as the wind howled through the slit around the sill. "I hope we're not too late to save the cottage."

Making sure her tool belt was secure around her waist, Hannah put her hand on the doorknob. She could feel the wind trying to get in. Getting outside would be tricky. Walking upwind would be difficult.

Sharon held her hammer in her hand and nodded.

When Hannah opened the door, the wind shoved it out of her hand and banged it against the wall, leaving a hole in the sheetrock. Blasting its way into the cottage, it sent the sheets flying around like ghosts. The hood on her raincoat was blown off her head. There was no time to worry about it. Work had to be done.

She grabbed Sharon's wrist and leaned forward into the gale. Rain pelted them under the porch. The porch swing continued its macabre dance, twisting and writhing like it wanted free of its chains. In a self-destructive arc, it hit the stone of the cottage wall, splintering what was left of the armrest.

Shouting and motioning into the violent wind, Hannah tried to tell Sharon she intended to climb on the railing, but her voice was swept away by the ferocious wind. She pounded the rail top and pointed at herself. Pointing at Sharon, she motioned lifting the swing enough to get the chain off the hook.

Sharon nodded. Her eyes were almost closed trying to keep the rain from getting in them. Her short gray hair was already soaked, plastered against her head.

Hannah envied Sharon's short hair dancing on her nodding head. The wind used her ponytail like a whip slashing against her face. A few strands broke free to slap her as if trying to free themselves from the roots. As the wind clawed at her raincoat, the rain and sand pelted her like thousands of BBs. Every cell in her body screamed out for her to leave and find shelter.

Fighting the gale, she gingerly climbed onto the wet railing, clinging to the support beam to keep from being blown off. With her free hand, she brushed the hair out of her eyes so she could see what she was doing. It was a futile effort so she moved her arm back and forth until it hit the moving chain holding the swing.

Standing in the hazardous spot between the house and the swing, Sharon braced her arms against the swing to keep it from bashing her. Using a knee as leverage, she lifted the end a few inches, giving slack in the chain.

Hannah reached out with her free hand and slipped the link off the hook. A gust of wind caught the swing and wrenched it out of Sharon's hands. The chain yanked in Hannah's hand, almost toppling her from the railing. One end of the swing fell with a thud on the porch.

Holding onto the porch's support beam, Hannah managed to find her balance on top of the railing. Hannah slid down and checked Sharon to make sure she wasn't hurt. A strong gust pushed the sisters against the front window, reminding them not to dilly dally.

Climbing the railing on the other side was trickier. The wind buffeted Hannah so hard she could hardly let go of the pillar to reach out for the chain. Hooking one leg around the pillar, she stood one-legged on the rail and reached out to the hook. The full weight of the swing was on this hook, making it harder for Sharon to lift it up. After several failed attempts to lift it, Sharon shook her arms out and gave a mighty heave. The chain went slightly limp but not enough to lift the link over the hook.

Taking a risk, Hannah let go of the pillar with her hand and yanked upward on the chain at the same time Sharon strained to lift it up. The extra energy allowed her to slip the chain from the hook and let the chain fall to the porch. Sharon jumped back and dropped the swing to the decking.

Fighting the winds pushing her, Hannah crawled off the railing and held on to Sharon while she caught her breath. The women were soaked by the rain and battered by the wind, but there was still work to do.

Hannah looked behind the shutter beside the large window, unloosed the latch, and let the wind bang it into place. One down, fifteen to go. While Sharon handled the other shutter, she pulled out the hammer and nailed the first one into place. A few swings of the hammer by Sharon had the second shutter nailed shut. She pointed to the other window and the two stumbled and battled against the wind to make their way to it.

The storm roared around the cottage like a kraken set on destruction, putting an exclamation point on their decision to board up the cottage. They'd waited too long.

Chapter 5

Essie

The Bunny household was quiet except for soft voices emanating through bedroom doors. The sun was down, and the kids were shut in their bedrooms doing homework or reading. Easter was somewhere, but she didn't care where as long as he wasn't bugging her. Quiet hour was in effect as per house rules. It was her favorite time of the day.

Her normal quiet time was troubling for her. Something in her mind kept poking at her brain, refusing to turn off so she could meditate. Giving up, she let her mind wander to what was causing her unease. Her sisters.

Rising, she took her laptop into the den and curled up in a recliner. Sitting in the dark made her feel hidden from the world and its troubles. Turning the computer on would allow them entry to her solitude. It was hard to give it up.

Logging in, she pulled up a US weather map with the latest news release about the Category 5 hurricane about to hit the Sarasota area of Florida. If the projected path of the storm was correct, there was a bullseye on her mother's cottage. The house was made of stone, but with a fourteen-foot storm surge expected, it might wash away, taking the clock with it. And taking away the last opportunity of seeing her mother.

Closing the website, she turned away and buried her face in her hands. Her family was her first priority, just like her mother had taught her. Once her family's needs were met, she could attend to her own needs. That time wouldn't come for another eleven years when the youngest would leave. Her thirteen highly intelligent, very active children kept her running from one thing to another almost every minute of every day. On top of everything else, she helped Easter with the factory when he needed her. Everybody needed a piece of her time, but there wasn't enough to parcel out. She was over-obligated.

Still, the storm was a hard reminder that not everything waits until a convenient time. For the clock, time may have run out. She hadn't tried hard enough to coordinate her schedule for the last visit with her mother. It might not only deprive her of another visit but deprive her children as well. And her sisters and their families. The guilt lay on her like a lead weight.

Slamming her laptop shut, the darkness contrasted with the fire she felt inside. She shrugged the guilt off her shoulders. It was Hannah's fault. She should have gone to take care of the cottage despite her not being able to help. There were companies she could have hired to board up the cottage for them. Or she could have called the ghost hunter friends who helped them with the cottage when it was haunted. She could have offered them a fee to do it. Her mother left enough money behind to take care of those kinds of things.

There was no doubt. It was Hannah's fault. She was unreasonable to expect Essie to interrupt her life to do something that could be contracted out. If she'd been smart, she'd have snapped to the cottage to get the money out of the hiding place—

Jerking upright, Essie almost dropped the laptop on the floor. The money! It was hidden in the closet in her mother's cottage. If the storm surge was as high as forecasted, it would wash away the money their mother left behind to take care of the cottage. They'd have nothing to pay taxes with or to rebuild the cottage. Without their mother's money, it would come out of their pockets, and hers were empty most of the time. They'd have to sell whatever was left of their childhood home. Without the cottage, the land might not be worth much. They'd be left with nothing.

Urgency pushed her out of her chair. Counting on her fingers, it was about two-thirty in the afternoon in Florida. She'd have to hurry if she was going to beat the storm surge to her mother's cottage.

Her bedroom door squeaked as she opened and shut it, announcing to the house one of the parents was going to bed. Dressing in the illumination of a nightlight, she quickly threw on a pair of jeans and a lavender tee shirt. Hannah would be disappointed in her attire, but she wouldn't be there. Her talisman and the necklace her father left her completed her attire. She would leave a note for Easter on his side of the bed.

A light came on behind her. She gasped and spun around to see Easter stretched out on the bed.
Unused to the brightness, he blinked until his eyes adjusted to the light. He pulled out his earbuds and said, "Sneaking out? If one of the children did that, they'd be mopping floors all week."

Her eyes rolled and her stress level rose with them. "This is serious. I have to go to Florida to get Mother's money before the storm hits." She looked for shoes to wear in the bottom of her closet.

Scrambling off the bed, he rushed to her and grabbed her arm. "Florida! Oh no, you're not."

Holding her shoes in one hand, she pulled free and tried to leave. He grabbed her shirt tail and pulled her back so he could reach her arm again.

Essie fought against him, but he held it firm. "Oh yes, I am! I'm not letting our money blow away. We need it for the cottage."

Easter's grip grew firmer and his voice louder. "You can't go now. It's too late. The money may already be scattered to the four winds."

His eyes gleamed with his fierce determination. She was as determined as he was. With her free arm, she grabbed the talisman around her neck. "I'm going. If you don't want to come with me, you better let go." Getting no sign of release, she started chanting, "Pop my bubble, I'm—"

With a yank, he threw her onto the bed and his hand went over her mouth, cutting her words off. His mouth was by her ear when he said, "I said no. The storm is already destructive. I don't want you in it."

Twisting, she pushed him away, sat up, and continued her chant. "I'mintroubletakemethereonthedouble." She took a breath to say her intended destination, but Easter beat her to it as he held her close.

"To our kitchen!"

In the split second after he said it, Essie blurted out, "Our kitchen? N—"

Her words were cut short when the spinning began and the pressure squeezed her. The tile floor went sliding under her backside as the two of them slid beside the lower cabinets. When they came to a stop, she flailed her arms to get free of Easter and stand up. Her hand went out to catch the edge of the cabinet to steady herself, except her hand went too far and grabbed hold of the apple strudel someone had left out. As Easter struggled, he hit her arm. Up went the strudel in its glass dish, making an arc before it crashed and shattered on the floor next to them. Her favorite baking dish lay in shards on the tile floor, and the strudel covered them, the cabinets, and the floor.

"Look what you did!" she shouted at Easter more out of frustration than a sense of loss. Her plan to save her mother's money was being completely thwarted by her stubborn husband. He was being totally unreasonable.

Strudel covered her lap. She grabbed a handful and threw it in Easter's face. "Look what you've done!"

Wiping strudel from his eyes, he responded in kind, "I didn't do this! You did! And it doesn't matter. You're still not going!" He flung strudel back at her.

A scream of frustration jumped past her lips. "When you have to pay for repairs to the cottage, you'll be sorry you didn't let me go!" She shoved him to make her point.

He pushed her back. "You're the stubborn one! Why don't you ever listen to—"

The kitchen light came on like a spotlight on a duo at a concert. Blinking and squinting, they heard the gasps and snickering of their offspring.

Holding her hand over her eyes, she growled, "Who left the strudel out?"

A chorus of tattletales sang out, "Alan!"

Without looking at her errant boy, she said, "Alan, you'll mop the kitchen floor every night for a month."

Tears filled Alan's eyes and he wailed, "I was hungry so I took some to bed. When I heard the noise, I dropped my plate of strudel in my bed."

Shutting her eyes, Essie wanted to disappear. The argument with Easter about the storm was wreaking havoc in her home. The cottage might be in shambles, but her house was too. Since she was here, the cleaning-up chores might as well get started.

She moved to get up, but Easter held her in place.

"Don't move," he said, "you might get cut by glass or slip and break something else. Pete, Marcia, go get a broom and a mop and get this cleaned up before blood is drawn. Sylvie and Clara, help them. The rest of you, help Alan get strudel out of his bed. Then all of you, get back to bed. You have school tomorrow."

Moans issued as the crowd broke up. Essie watched as an apple slice slowly slid down Easter's cheek. She was about to break out laughing when she heard a small voice, "Are you and Papa getting divorced?" Ned's small eyes peeked around the edge of the doorway.

"No!" Essie said more earnestly than she intended. "Why would you say that?"

"Look at you," Sue pointed at them. "We'd get in SO much trouble if we had a food fight."

Taking a breath to compose herself, she continued, "This was an accident. Ned, just because Mama and Papa disagree doesn't mean they are getting a divorce. It means they...disagree. No more of this silly talk about divorce. Go back to your room. Read for a few minutes. Papa will check on you later."

"Mama will check on you too," Easter said as he gave Essie a warning shot with his eyes.

She stared at her husband as he wiped the apple slice away. How had she let it get so out of control? The money was nothing compared to her family's security. Their loud argument about it had frightened her son into thinking he was losing his parents. Shame washed away the anger she'd felt at Easter.

Pete came back with a broom and started sweeping at the entrance to the kitchen. "Care to tell us what was going on?"

Behind him with a mop, Marcia piped in, "Yeah. You know how embarrassing it is to find your parents wrestling in strudel on the kitchen floor? Aren't the two of you too old for this kind of thing?"

Easter wiped more strudel off his face. "A word of advice to everyone!" He raised his voice so all could hear. "Save yourself a little embarrassment and keep this incident to yourself. No one needs to know about this."

With a sly look as he swept up the apples and glass shards, Pete said, "It might cost you a tank of gas in my car." Making a wide sweep, he cleared away a path for them to get out of the kitchen.

"Don't push your luck," Easter said as he rose. He extended a hand to Essie and pulled her up. "I think I need a shower. And so do you."

As she left with her now-forgiven husband, Essie called out behind her, "Thanks for cleaning up the mess, kids. I consider it payback for all the times I cleaned up after you."

The warm water in the shower felt good on her body, but it didn't wash the worry away. Easter might not care if the money blew away, but she did. Somehow, someway she had to get to the cottage to get it. The problem was, Easter had taken her talisman and swore he wouldn't give it back until the storm had passed. By then it would be too late to recover the money. The only option she had left was to go crawling to Hannah and ask her to go check on the money.

Her fingers scrubbed her scalp hard, tangling her shoulder-length hair into a knotted mess. After applying a dab of conditioner and rinsing, she cranked off the water and got out. Quickly drying, she found a robe and sat on the bed with her phone and dialed Hannah.

A strange voice came into her ear, telling her Hannah was not available but to leave a message. She didn't want to leave a message. She wanted an answer. Sharon might know what was going on. She quickly hung up and called Sharon but had the same unanswered response. Her fingertips drummed out the tempo of her impatience on top of the phone as it sat in her lap.

Maybe Headless would answer. He intimidated her even though he'd been nothing but polite to her. As far as she knew, he was only scary one night a year. Every Halloween, the anniversary of him losing his head, he terrorized the neighborhood in anger. Astride his large black stallion, his eyes blazing red and his mouth deforming into the jagged grin of a jack-o-lantern, he raced along quiet roads and through the cemetery, chasing whoever happened to be passing that way.

Other than that, he was a kind man.

She scrolled through her contact list but didn't find him. Maybe Santa could call Hannah or Headless for her, if she had his number.

As she scrolled back through her list, her phone rang. An unknown number displayed, piquing her interest. She debated on whether to answer or not. Scammer calls annoyed her to no end, and she usually ignored calls from numbers she didn't know. While she mulled her options, her finger went unbidden to the answer button and hit it before she could stop it. She stared unbelieving at her phone.

"Hello?" Her voice sounded squeaky and unused. She cleared her throat.

A voice came through. "Hello? Anyone there?"

Essie blinked as she recognized the voice of Headless. "Y—Yes," she stammered. "Headless? Is that you?"

"Yes!" A sigh of relief came across the miles. "I'm glad I got you. Are you busy? Can you talk?"

"It's almost nine-thirty at night here. My children are in their rooms, getting ready to go to sleep, I hope. I was just thinking of you. What's going on there? Did Hannah get to the cottage?"

She listened as Headless told how Sharon snapped in, and she and Hannah decided to go close the shutters on the house before the worst of the storm hit. They'd been gone longer than he thought they should be and was worried. Something might have gone wrong. He was about to use his talisman to snap there to check on them and help with whatever problem was taking so long. He'd left a note for the boys telling them he'd be back soon.

His problem gave her an idea. If she went to Florida instead of him, she could see about the money. She could snap into the cottage, out of the storm and wind, check on the money and her sisters. She'd be back before the children got up in the morning. Surely Easter would return her talisman when he found out they needed her help. "Let me go check on them. I don't mind. And you'll be home when your boys come. Give me half an hour to get ready and let Easter know you need my help."

With a tone of worry, Headless breathed out, "But the storm. It's bad—"

"No worries. I'll stay inside the cottage. Thanks, Headless, I'll let you know what I find out." She hung up and went to find Easter. It would take her only a few minutes to gather the money. If her sisters were still there, she'd help them and together they could rescue the money. It was what Hannah had been asking for…for her to come. Hannah may hound on her about not coming sooner, but right or wrong, it was too late to change what had happened. Headless and her sisters needed her help, and she was happy to spend a few nighttime hours to do it.

She found Easter in the kitchen cleaning the last of their strudel mishap from the cabinet fronts. The broom and dustpan sat nearby. Marcia and Pete were gone, either remiss in their cleaning duties or dismissed by their father.

"Easter, I have to go to Hannah's. Headless called and he asked me to come help out." So it wasn't exactly the truth; her account made it a better story.

He wiped the cabinets with more vigor. "Why?"

As he rose to rinse his rag out in the sink, she took a step back. "Hannah and Sharon went to the cottage to board it up before the storm hit and they haven't returned. He's worried and wants to check on them. He can't leave home right now so he asked if I'd check on them."

The muscles in his jaw twitched and quivered. "Headless called, huh. Sounds like the perfect ruse to get there." He wrung every drop of moisture out of the rag he was using. Pressing his lips tight together, words pried them slightly apart. "You're determined to go, aren't you."

Essie felt her jaw muscles start moving as she clenched her teeth. She met his stony gaze with one of her own. "I don't appreciate being called a liar."

"I didn't call you a liar. I'm calling your bluff."

"I'm not bluffing!" Her hands moved to her hips. "Feel free to call Headless yourself and ask if he made the request. When he tells you he did, you can eat the words you're flinging at me."

Turning away, he spread the mostly dry rag out across the countertop, smoothing it out like he was ironing it. "Why can't Headless leave home? It makes more sense if you should stay at the Horseman house and let him go to the cottage. If they need help, he'll be better able to do it."

"But he said he couldn't go. What else am I supposed to do? Tell him you won't let me come help?"

Easter crossed his arms. "You're not getting your talisman back until you promise me you won't to go to the cottage."

"What if I promise to stay inside the cottage? It'll protect me from the storm."

He shook his head. "Not good enough. Go take care of the boys and let Headless go check on them if he wants to. The storm is destructive, and you don't need to be in it. I don't want my kids growing up without a mother."

A wave of guilt swept over her. No amount of money was worth getting hurt in a storm. She didn't like the terms but had no other choice than to make an X over her heart. "I promise."

He rubbed at the worry wrinkles on his forehead. "Fine. Go. Just come back in one piece."

He reached in his pocket and pulled out the talisman. It swung between them like the pendulum on her father's clock. She reached up and felt the necklace her father left for her on their last visit to the cottage. If the clock was destroyed by the storm, it might be the only thing she had left of her parents.

Her hand went out for the talisman. "I will."

When the spinning and squeezing stopped, Essie found herself in the middle of a living room with leather and wood décor. Large paintings of horses lined the walls. If this was Hannah's home, it was a pleasant surprise from how Essie expected her home to appear. It was homey…inviting. Her home was more eclectic. Whatever was comfortable. Whatever she could afford. Hannah's place was put together like something out of a magazine. A little green-eyed monster inside Essie stirred slightly.

"Essie!"

She turned to see her brother-in-law coming toward her with a crooked grin on his face. With one hand steadying his head, he hugged her and welcomed her to his home. "I'm glad you came, but I thought you were going to Florida. I didn't expect you here."

With an eyeroll and a flick of her wrist, she explained. "Easter made me promise I wouldn't go there. He said you should."

The grin disappeared. "I guess that will work. I'm worried about Hannah and Sharon and thought they might need help. Want coffee before I go?"

Back home, it was past her bedtime, long after she normally drank caffeine of any kind. With the time change, she might grow sleepy when she was needed most. Coffee might keep her eyes open for a few more hours or at least until she returned home. She nodded and followed him to the large immaculate kitchen. The green-eyed monster nudged her again, but she pushed it away.

"No word from Hannah or Sharon yet?"

Headless pushed a mug of coffee toward her, then brought creamer and sugar. He looked at the clock over the oven. "It's been over three hours ago. I didn't expect them to be gone but an hour or two at most. I'm watching the storm on the internet, and it's getting more intense by the minute. They should be back by now."

Taking a sip of coffee, she asked, "Why didn't you go help them?"

His dark eyes stared at her long enough to give her the willies. He pointed at his head. "I've never faced hurricane winds since...." A faraway look passed across his eyes before he blinked several times. "The wind would blow my head off and roll it down the beach." He slapped the countertop with his hand, making Essie jump. "I will forever rue the day I didn't duck when I saw the cannonball coming for me."

Unsure of how to react to his confession and outburst, she quickly took a drink of coffee, hoping it wouldn't burn her tongue.

His face brightened. "But…" he waved his finger in the air. "I figured out a way to go without losing it." He pointed at his chest. "I'll wear this hoodie and tie the strings tightly around my face. Doing that should keep it in place, don't you think?"

Modern innovations had saved the day. "I think that's brilliant!"

As he was tightening the hood's string to hold his head on, a familiar snap sounded from the living room. They rushed in to see a sopping wet Hannah standing there. Her long hair was knotted and wrapped around her pale, wind-whipped face. Her clothes were wet and smelled of saltwater. Water dripped and formed a puddle around her feet. She teetered right before Headless reached her, and she slumped into his arms. He helped her to a chair at the table.

"Honey!" Headless cried out. "What happened? Where's Sharon?"

She wiped her face off with her hands. "She's coming. I'm surprised she didn't beat me here." She panted as if she'd run a race. Pausing in her efforts to hold the water out of her eyes, she sputtered, "Essie, what are you doing here?"

Feeling her jaw working without words coming out, Essie pointed at Headless.

"I asked her to come," he replied for her.

With a shrug and a wave of her hand, Hannah dismissed her sister. "Can you get me a towel, sweetheart?" she asked Headless as she wrung her tresses.

Gone only an instant, Headless was back with towels. He gently rubbed her hair with one as she dried her arms.

The digital numbers on the stove changed three times, and there was still no sign of Sharon. Essie's heart began to pound thinking about her alone in the storm. "I thought you said she was coming."

Still dripping, Hannah ran a towel across her torso. "We agreed to come back."

Panic was beginning to rise in Essie. "But she didn't. That means you left her there. What were you thinking? She'll start panicking, and no one will be there to help her!"

Wiping the hair away from her face, she replied, "Maybe she went home instead of coming here. She had her hand on the talisman when I left."

Headless used the towel to mop the floor as he asked, "Tell us what happened."

Hannah took a deep breath as she ran a towel through her hair. "We got the porch swing taken down and the shutters nailed shut. The wind was so fierce we could barely move in it. The rain felt like pellets being shot out of a gun. It hurt! Once we got the shutters secured, we went inside to move things off the floor and figure out some way to protect the clock. We set the clock to five to slow time outside the cottage so we could get everything done. We got a few things put up, but when I looked outside, the surf was lapping at the front porch. The storm surge was coming in."

Something didn't make sense to Essie. Time alterations still baffled her. Her brain hadn't thought about the concept in so long the idea seemed fuzzy. It took her a long minute to get it straight in her mind. "But if the clock was set to five, wouldn't that have slowed how fast the water came up?"

"I thought so. Time should have stopped outside, meaning the storm wasn't moving as fast. That's what it did when we set it to five before. But the oddest thing was the clock worked. We set it to five o'clock and when I checked it later, it said five-thirty."

The statement stunned Essie. The clock worked magically but never mechanically. It should have stayed at five o'clock no matter how long it ran. "The storm might have messed the vibes up or something. Or maybe it doesn't work in bad weather."

"That's ridiculous. The weather doesn't matter." Toweling off her arms and legs, Hannah added, "All I know is the storm surge came up fast. Faster than we thought it would. When I left, the roof was creaking and popping. I was afraid it would blow off any second."

Headless wrapped the extra towel around Hannah's shoulders. He looked in the living room. "Sharon's still not here. We need to make sure she got out. If not, we need to get her out of there."

A dark look passed over Hannah's face. "She wanted to call Father back. I kept telling her no, but she kept insisting we should. I thought we'd settled the matter, but I bet she stayed to call him. He never comes right away, and I didn't want him to arrive during the storm. Besides, the storm was getting worse and worse." She stopped drying herself. "You don't think she's still there waiting on Father?"

Kneeling in front of Hannah, Headless grabbed her arms. "Why didn't you grab her and force her to come back with you? You know she wasn't in great shape when you left."

Hannah glared at Essie and Headless. "Ever try to get one of the Time girls to do something they didn't want to do?"

Somewhere between her heart beating loudly in her ears and the icy cold she felt inside, Essie's logical side peeked its head up. "If conditions were as bad as you say, Sharon likely snapped herself home. She could get cleaned up and put on dry clothes before coming here." Her insides relaxed a little. "I bet she went home."

Hannah took the towel from Headless and ran it through her hair one last time. Throwing down the towel, she said, "Somebody call Santa and see if she's there. I'm going back to get her if she isn't." She took a wobbly step or two to the middle of the floor.

Pulling out her phone, Essie found Santa's number and pushed the button. He answered quickly but said he hadn't seen Sharon. He'd look around their house to see if she snapped in somewhere unseen. With worry filling his voice, he urged her to call if they found her.

Headless and Hannah stared at her as she shook her head. Nothing had to be said. They knew Sharon was in trouble.

Headless tied the hood's string tighter around his face. "I'll go check the cottage. She's probably there. I'll get her back with or without her cooperation." He pulled his talisman out of his pocket, recited the chant, and was gone.

Wobbling, Hannah made her way to the bedroom to change. Essie sat at the table, her own insides agitating like a washing machine. Sharon needed to be here. Where she was safe. Hannah was right. There wasn't time to call their father and expect him to come immediately. If Sharon wasn't at home, she might be paralyzed by a bad panic attack, probably brought on by the rising tide. Too scared to leave and too scared to stay.

As much as she didn't want to acknowledge it, Easter had been right to insist she not go to the cottage. From what Hannah said, the extreme danger would be too much for her to handle. Headless had the strength to force Sharon to come back with him. He'd take care of her.

"Could you get me a cup of coffee?" Hannah called as she returned in a robe. Her legs still wobbled a little, making her walk in a crooked line.

Her request helped Essie stop imagining the worst possible outcomes. She hurried to the cabinet where she'd seen Headless fetch a mug. Pouring the last of the coffee from the pot into the mug, she brought it back to Hannah.

Watching her sister lift the warm mug to her lips with shaking hands, Essie wondered how to ask the question heavy on her mind. Hannah hadn't returned with a backpack or bundle. That meant the money was still there, probably being washed away as they drank their coffee. Unless it was why Sharon hadn't returned. Maybe she thought of it and would bring it back with her.

The timing for the question wasn't good, but she had to know the answer. With a pounding heart, Essie asked, "Does Sharon have the money out of the closet?"

Hannah gave her a hard stare as she took another sip. "Is that all you're worried about? The money?"

"N—no. I just wondered—"

"The money is safe in a bank."

Essie watched as Hannah looked away and ran her fingers through her wet hair. Essie oscillated between being happy the money was safe and angry about her flippant attitude about it. Her answer had birthed multiple questions. Why was it in the bank? When was it put there? Who knew about it? Their mother had left money for the care of her cottage. Since Essie was the eldest, why hadn't she heard about this? She should know what was going on. But first things first. "How did it get to the bank?"

Hannah gripped the mug with both hands. "I put it in there. A little at a time so no government report had to be submitted. It's easier to pay taxes and homeowners insurance with a bank account than with cash."

Her roiling mind pushed Essie to her feet. "You went to the cottage without telling me? I thought we agreed not to go unless we all go."

Hannah's eye roll was like one her daughters used on her, and it aggravated Essie just as much.

Staring at Essie, Hannah explained. "How do you think the bills were paid? Out of my money? I paid the taxes, insurance, and utilities. Sometimes I paid Jeff Campbell to make sure no ghosts or squatters had resettled in the cottage. I took care of the place and doing so requires money. So yes, I put it in the bank so it was accessible and easy to use. I went there several times to get it all."

Essie paced. "And who has access to the money? Just you?"

"For now. Since you never have time for anything having to do with the cottage, I haven't done anything with the bank account. I can put yours and Sharon's names on the account, but we'll have to go to the bank together to do it." She leaned forward. "Don't you trust me?"

It was a trick question. Essie left it hovering between them unanswered. Pacing was the only release for Essie's anger. The money was safe, but how much of it was left? Should she insist on an audit? The demand seemed a little farfetched, but it was perfectly justifiable. She and Sharon deserved to know where their parts of their mother's money was, how it was spent, whether it was in the bank or in Hannah's pocket.

A fearful whine came from Hannah as she rose from the table and joined in the pacing. "He should be back by now. I hope Sharon's okay. If she fights him, Headless will pick her up and come back. If Father came, he'll tell her to leave. He knows how bad the storm will be." She teetered slightly and returned to her seat. "They should be here soon, don't you think?" She tapped her fingertips against her crossed arms.

The bucket of reality cooled Essie's anger. The money was secondary to Sharon's safety. She sat at the table and held on to Hannah's hands. "I'm sure Headless can handle any situation. They should be here any second."

Chapter 6

Sharon

Sharon was relieved when Hannah left the cottage, leaving her to do what she had to do. She didn't want to hear what couldn't or shouldn't be done. Someone had to take care of the magical clock and who better than Father. She quickly set the clock to twelve and pushed the pendulum.

A loud crack sounded above the howling of the fierce winds, and the cottage trembled in fear. Sharon's hair stood on end like it was being sucked upward. A thin line of light flashed between the ceiling and the walls, then disappeared. Not much time was left. The storm was tearing the cottage apart.

Her heart pounded. Curling into a fetal position on the leather sofa, she yelled into the booming storm. "Father, where are you? Come quickly! You have to save the clock!"

She'd done the best she could to protect it. The plastic shower curtain from the bathroom was draped around the bottom of the clock. Desperate to do more, she raced into the kitchen to get a box of plastic wrap. Throwing the box aside, she wound the tube of thin plastic around the base of the clock. It might not keep the water out, but it wouldn't hurt. Round and round she went with it until she reached the clock face. It read ten minutes after twelve.

She stood frozen, wondering what was wrong. The clock had never read that time. It had never kept human time. In the midst of the storm, when she needed it to work its magic the most, it was working like it was a regular clock. Something was wrong.

There was no time to think it through. The cottage shuddered in its death throes. With a mighty crack, the ceiling disappeared into the storm. Wind strafed the interior, and rain gushed in like a faucet on a bathtub. Water beat against the shutters. The front door groaned before a strong wave pushed it in. Water invaded the living room that held so many memories, washing them aside as it moved into the kitchen and hallway.

Sharon screamed out as the forces of nature pushed her against the clock. She clung to it with all her might. Her only thought was saving the clock. It was her only connection to her parents. She couldn't let it go.

"Father, where are you?"

Parts of the house began to be plucked out by their roots and fly away in the wind. As the wall buckled, the clock began to teeter. Turning her back to it, she tried to steady it, but her strength was too little. It fell on her with a crash, knocking her to her stomach. Salty water covered her face as the clock pinned her to the floor. She pushed and writhed, but the clock was too heavy to move off her. Panic swelled in her. Most of her oxygen was gone. She needed to suck in a breath but fought the urge.

Out of strength and out of air, she lay still, accepting her fate. Santa would be cross with her for staying at the cottage too long. Martha would be stuck doing the cooking. Who would help Santa with the good and naughty lists?

She wished her father had heard her call. Hannah had been right. He wouldn't come in time. For the first time ever, he'd disappointed her.

Water caressed her face, seducing her to suck it into her lungs. Blackness swirled around her, ready to swallow her.

As the last atom of oxygen was used in her lungs, the heavy weight holding her down lifted. She smiled. Father had finally come for her.

Strong hands grabbed her and pulled her face out of the water. They wiped her face gently and slapped her cheek. Taking in a big breath she sucked in air and drops of water. A coughing fit shook her body as she felt strong hands lift her to a sitting position.

Someone bent over her as she coughed and held her tight. A man's voice barely came through the storm. "Hang on. I'll get you out of here."

Her panic subsided as she released her weakness to him. "I knew you'd come, Father. You saved me." Everything went black again.

Sharon's head swirled. The whole world was spinning, and she dared not open her eyes. Garbled voices wafted in the air around her like the aroma from a scented candle. Her skin felt funny, tingly with pain, pricking her here and there. Nothing on her body seemed to work. She was nothing more than a rag doll being tended to by others. Someone gently laid her on a hard, wet surface. A hand cradled the back of her head until it softly touched down.

"Thank you, Father," she whispered. "I knew you'd help me."

Strange hands touched her, sparking more flashes of pain. She wanted to push them away but couldn't move. Her nose started to itch, but her hand wouldn't move that far. The lack of control over her body made her blood stir with anxiety as a full-blown panic attack threatened to sweep her away. Her breath came quickly which made her hurt more.

"You're safe now, Sharon," Hannah's soft voice came through her fear. "Here's a paper bag. I'll help you breathe into this."

A bag was opened and put over her face and mouth. The familiar paper crinkling sound helped her panic levels subside, and her head quit spinning. Peeking out of one eye, she saw Headless leaning over her, his soaked hood still tight around his crooked face. Its unnatural look didn't help her anxiety. Until he moved it to look natural, she'd keep her eyes closed. If she looked as bad as he did, she must be a sight.

She listened for her father's voice but didn't hear it. He must be watching them help her.

"Where's Father?" Her voice felt and sounded raspy inside the paper bag. She fought the urge to cough. It would hurt too much.

The bag was pulled back. "He's not here," Hannah said as she wiped Sharon's face with a towel.

"But he saved me," Sharon said, desperately wanting to believe it. "I called him, and he came. He saved the clock and me. He was there. I know it."

Hannah looked at Headless leaning over her and let out an oh-brother sigh. "I told you she'd stayed behind to call him. Of all the—"

"Your father wasn't there," Headless said like the gentle soul he was. "I was the one who lifted the clock off of you and brought you here."

"But I called him." A lump in her throat made it hard for her to swallow. A coughing fit racked her as a tear ran down the side of her face. An aching in her side made her uncomfortable. She tried to rise but found no strength to do it. Resting a moment, she regathered what strength she could and tried again. Headless put his hand under her back and helped her sit up in the puddle on the floor around her.

A soft snap sounded right before a voice more precious than any other sounded nearby. "Thank you for bringing me, Essie," Santa said. "It was faster than the sled, but much more dizzifying."

A rustling of clothes and popping knees brought him close to Sharon's side. "I'm here with you, Sharon. I'll take care of you."

Santa's voice immediately calmed her. Her beloved husband was with her. Most of her fear left, leaving her to soak in his comfort and love. The tingling inside her slowed as she felt his hands squeeze hers, and her breathing returned to normal. Opening her eyes a crack, Santa's twinkling eyes hovered above hers, his rosy lips curled into a smile.

"You scared me, sweetheart," he whispered. He stroked her hair away from her face. "What were you thinking? Staying in the storm, I mean—"

Bending over Santa, Hannah pointed her finger at Sharon as she declared, "You should have listened to me!" Headless pulled her back.

A frown covered Santa's face as his beard moved in cadence with his jaw muscles. A forced smile appeared next. "Honey, you should have come back sooner. You wouldn't have gotten hurt that way."

Stirring, Sharon felt strength slowly coming back into her limbs, bringing with it aches and pains. "I had to call Father to save the clock. He came, didn't he? The clock is saved, isn't it?" She touched her forehead while her memory dug through files. "What happened after Father came?"

"You don't remember?" Santa looked up at Headless. With a flick of his wrist, he invited Headless to kneel beside him.

Leaning over her, Headless had pushed his hood back and straightened his head, making it easier for Sharon to look at him. "You were hurt in your mother's cottage. The clock fell on you, pinning you underwater. You were about to drown. I'm glad I got there in time."

The words made no sense. Sharon had called her father and he came. He lifted the clock off her and saved her. She stared into her brother-in-law's eyes full of pity and worry. Looking away, her heart ached, and her body went cold.

Headless stood, leaving Santa alone beside her. He brushed away a solitary tear running down her face. "Headless saved you, sweetheart. Hear me? It wasn't your father. It was Headless who saved you. Brought you back. Out of the storm. You're safe and sound now." He kissed her forehead and circled his arms around as best he could.

The past few hours came back to her. Going with Hannah to shutter the cottage. The fierce wind and rain. Struggling to stay on her feet as they went around the cottage, nailing the shutters closed. Going inside and seeing the clock read nine-fifteen. Needing her father to help save the clock. Hannah saying there was no time and her leaving. The roof being pulled off the cottage like the lid to a can. Water coming in everywhere.

Most of all, she remembered the clock. She tried to save it. Her father could have saved it. Why hadn't he come when she called him? Disappointment washed through like the storm surge assaulting the cottage.

She closed her eyes again, trying to hide from what she knew to be true already. "What happened to the clock?"

"We don't know," Hannah replied in a piteous tone. "It's too dangerous for anyone to go check on it." She brought a chair for Santa to sit on.

Santa sat and pulled her close to his leg while he stroked her hair with a towel. "Don't you worry about the clock. You did all you could do."

Her insides cringed and gripped her. His words held the answer to her question. The clock was gone. She would never see her father or mother again. For the second time, she'd lost them. The ache in her sides grew as the tears started running along the sides of her face. She wanted to stop the pain in her side, but the pain in her heart was greater and she couldn't control it. She sobbed, releasing her anguish out loud.

With more rustling, knee popping, and grunts, Santa sat on the floor with her and pulled her to him. "Don't worry, sweetheart. It may still be there. When it's safe, we'll go back and look for it. We can take the clock to our shop and make it new again. Don't cry. Godfrey can fix it."

It was true. Godfrey was an old elf who worked on the most delicate and complex toys. His mechanical abilities were superb. His workshop had tools of every kind. He could take the clock apart, dry it out, and put it back together again. Once a new roof and other repairs were made to the cottage, Santa could return the clock, and all would be normal again. They could call their mother and father again. Her pain eased, and the tears stopped.

"You could...do that...couldn't you?" Knowing there was a plan for the clock relieved her worry and let other thoughts crowd in. The overhead light bothered her eyes as she opened them wider. Blinking, she saw Santa wore his white work shirt and coveralls. "How did you get here so quickly?"

Santa held his forehead. "Essie brought me with her magical necklace. That's quite a ride!" With a groan and much effort, he stood up. "I called Elwin and asked him to bring the work sleigh here. I don't think I could take another squeezing-and-spinning."

"You told someone else about the talisman?" Hannah seemed freaked. "Mrs. Hagg isn't going to like that."

"Couldn't be helped," Santa told her. "He was there when Essie snapped in. Don't worry. We made him take a vow of secrecy. He's a good man and will keep his word. Besides, I needed help with excuses on why I was suddenly gone."

Sharon felt her body relax, and the pain eased. There was hope for the clock. "Can we go home?"

With the help of the other three, she got to her feet. Her legs wobbled but stiffened enough to hold her upright. She stood there with help beside the kitchen table as water dripped from her sweat suit like she'd come out of a swimming pool. "I think I need to change."

Essie suddenly appeared in front of her. "I can snap to your place and get you dry clothes."

"I think I have a suitcase somewhere around here. It has dry clothes in it."

Headless walked to the laundry room, his feet squishing in his shoes as he went.

Hannah brought towels and made dams around Sharon's feet to soak up the water. Her quick trip to the laundry room produced a mop and bucket. The puddle around her seemed to warrant sandbags to contain it. She instructed Headless to retreat to the laundry room to change into a pair of overalls before making his way to their shower to clean up.

"You can clean up in the boys' bathroom," Hannah directed Sharon. "Wrap these towels around you, and hurry so the carpet doesn't get too wet. I'll bring your suitcase to you."

With Santa's firm arm to hang on to, Sharon hurried as fast as she could on her unsteady legs across the living room and down the hall. With Santa's help, she sat on the edge of the tub and leaned against the wall. At her insistence, Santa went to join the others in the living room.

After resting a minute, she took off her wet sweat suit and crammed it into the sink. The outfit wasn't worth saving. A soft knock at the door and Santa's voice came telling her he had her suitcase. When he slid it in, she asked him to bring a garbage bag for her wet clothes.

The hot water in the shower felt good on her skin, pushing out the last of her tension. Grit and sand washed away out of her hair, and she felt restored to her whole self. Observing herself in the mirror as she dried off, a cut ran along the top of her eyebrow. Blue and purple bruises covered her ribs and arms. They ached as she moved her arms to slip on the blue blouse and black slacks. Her father's necklace still hung around her neck. She caressed the clock-face necklace, wishing she could move its hands to twelve. She needed her father's reassurance losing the clock was not her fault. She'd tried to save it.

And the talisman. Her image in the mirror showed where it was supposed to be but nothing was there. "Santa!" she screeched.

In a split second, Santa came bursting in the bathroom, wide-eyed and arms wide, ready to catch her. "What's wrong?"

"My talisman is gone!"

"Maybe it's in your clothes." He untied the garbage sack and emptied the clothes into the bathtub. Together they combed through the soggy fabric but found nothing.

"Maybe it went down the drain."

"No, the drain screen is too small for it to have passed through."

"When was the last time you used it?"

Sitting on the side of the tub, Sharon held her head in her hands. "I used it to go to the cottage. If I lost it there, it's gone forever. What am I going to tell Hannah? She'll be furious with me for losing it."

"Now, now, dear, don't fret." Santa pulled her hands away from her face. "Let's not tell her yet. It may turn up later when we've had time to think. We've got enough to worry about for now."

The aches started up again, inside and out. "But I need it to check on the clock after the storm is gone." Tears filled her eyes and overflowed onto her cheeks.

The talisman had been a blessing. The ability to move from place to place so quickly had spoiled her. It allowed her to see her childhood home one last time, although she could have died there. A shudder ran through her. People died in hurricanes. Headless had saved her from becoming one of the statistics, and she could never repay him for that. Maybe it was best it was gone. Without it, she couldn't get into trouble.

With nothing else to be done, Sharon collected the wet clothes, and put them back in the bag. Santa reassured her again it would turn up somewhere. He helped her clean up the bathroom before leaving it.

Essie and Hannah were visiting in the kitchen when Sharon and Santa walked in. Headless came in from the bedroom dressed in farm overalls and a shirt.

"Feel better?" Hannah asked.

Nodding, Sharon took the cup of hot tea offered and sat at the table where the others joined her. "I want to thank you, Headless, for coming after me. I wouldn't be sitting here if you hadn't. I'm so grateful it wasn't you at the cottage, Essie. If you had been, you'd have drowned. I'm sure of it. The ending would have been different. My dream would have come true." Her voice quivered and she sniffed.

The eyebrows on Essie's face reached for her hairline, but she didn't reply.

Santa patted her hand. "Sharon, dear, it was a dream, not an omen. The main thing is all is well, and all of you are safe and sound. Put it behind you."

"But your dream did come true," Headless said softly. "Didn't you tell Hannah you saw a form laying under the clock and another form lifting it? That happened, only it was you, not Essie."

Silence fell across the group like a blanket floating down. The realization he was right spread through those at the table. Inside Sharon, relief mingled with fear. She didn't want to have ESP.

Glancing at Santa, he shook his head with a tiny motion. "It was coincidence. You're not a seer." He pushed back from the table. "So, Headless, want to show me this farm of yours?"

Hannah pointed toward the back door. "Take him out to the barn. Nothing relaxes you more than taking care of your horses, and you need to relax." The last word was emphasized with a hard look. She turned to her sisters. "He had to postpone his customer's visit until tomorrow morning, but he didn't mind. With all this excitement, I'm glad he did. Plus, it gives him one more day to make sure the horses are in great condition for him."

An awkward silence fell. Chairs scraped against the floor as the two men stood. Headless cleared his throat, "You think your reindeer are great, wait until you see my horses." They hurried a little faster than normal to get out the door.

Essie checked her cell phone. "Look at the time! My children are in bed and probably asleep. They better be. They won't miss me so my secret treks are still secret. I'll have to be back before they get up or they'll know something is going on. I hope Easter will find a good excuse for me not being there."

"You didn't plan an alibi before you left?" Hannah asked in a snarky way.

"We weren't on the best of speaking terms when I left."

"You two have a fight?" Hannah asked.

A wiggle of the eyebrows and a smirk gave her answer. "Possibly. Never mind that. There's still one matter to discuss. The money. I'm not leaving until I know about the money."

Sharon's heart stopped. A deep gulp of air energized her voice. "Mother's money! I completely forgot about it. Mother's stash is gone. How will we pay the taxes?" The aches from her bruises returned as she started to cry and hold her ribs. How much worse could it get?

Chapter 7

Hannah

That did it. Hannah grabbed two handfuls of her hair and let out a scream topping Sharon's sobbing. She feigned pulling out her hair. The noise. The imposition. It needed to stop. There was no reason for this turmoil.

"Knock it off!" she cried out before her final scream. "The money is safe. It's in the bank."

Sharon's red-rimmed eyes stared at her. Essie scowled and started to say something, but rather than give her an opening, Hannah blocked it shut.

"For the past couple of years, I brought the money here and put it into a checking account and a savings account. That way I could easily pay the taxes and upkeep for the next five years. The rest of Mother's money is invested in CDs and in the money market earning interest. I will show you the statements. I called it the Francis Time Cottage Fund."

Essie stood up, hands on hips. "Who gave you permission to move the money? Or invest it? Why didn't you discuss it with us?" She waved a finger between her and Sharon.

Sharon wiped her eyes. "I thought we'd agreed to go to the cottage only when we all went. If you went without us, that's like…like cheating."

With her sisters lining up against her, Hannah wanted to snap somewhere quiet. She stared out the window beyond them, concentrating on one of their mares nursing its foal. The pastoral scene reminded her she was at home. The other two were intruders, close to becoming unwelcome intruders.

Pressing her teeth together hard enough to bite through steel, she found a trace of her civility. "Someone had to look after the place."

Sharon leaned forward. "You never asked us to help you."

Without taking her eyes off the mare and foal, she responded, "I asked for help before the storm and no one came." Neither sister said anything.

The battle was turning back her way. "I never knew when I'd have time to go so I went when I could. I spent an afternoon there every now and again. I'd enjoy a nice swim and check to make sure everything was in working order. I dusted and swept. Plus, I made sure none of Captain Fremont's crew or their friends returned."

"Did they?" Sharon asked slightly trembling.

"No. The house was empty. I worried about burglars breaking in and causing damage and even finding the money."

Sharon sniffed. "That's not something I thought about. I'm glad you went to check on the cottage."

Feeling more self-assured, Hannah added, "With each visit, I'd bring back some of the money and put it in the bank. Not enough the bank would have to fill out a report, but enough so that I eventually got it deposited without any suspicion."

Essie viewed her from the side of her narrowed eyes. "How much is in the bank? Are you keeping records of what you spend?"

"Of course, I am," Hannah spit out. Something clawed at her insides, threatening to turn ugly. She steeled herself against the threat. "I deposited about $440,000. I paid taxes on the cottage the past two years, plus the insurance, electricity, and utilities. The rest is in the bank earning interest." Taking a second look at her older sister's face, she added, "I'm not taking any for myself, if that's what you're implying."

Essie looked away. "Money does funny things to people. They suddenly get miserly and possessive. The least you could have done is told Sharon and I what you were doing. Why all the secrecy? Why, I knew this woman who...."

Heat flushed through Hannah's body so she looked out the window for a moment away from the mindless chatter. The colt had finished its meal and was frolicking while his mother grazed and swatted flies with her long tail. The mare's tail reminded her of how she was feeling as her sisters continued to voice their concerns over her handling the money. Accusations and leading questions circled about her like flies over roadkill. All she needed was something to swat them away with.

Her strategy of moving the money and telling them later seemed a good idea at the time. Underhandedness and theft had never entered her mind. The money was safer in a bank than in her mother's closet. That was her motivation and was the outcome. The hurricane was proving her point.

Her hands held up to deflect the barrage, she told her sister to hush. When they didn't, she said it louder. When Essie accused her of wanting the money to pay for her sons' college education, she lost her cool. "I think you should go home, Essie. Come back when you can talk to me rationally. And call before you come. I may be too busy to see you."

Essie crossed her arms. "I'll leave when I know Sharon is okay."

The sun was below the horizon when Hannah made her way to the barn. She leaned on the tall gates Headless had fashioned for the doors of the foaling room. Inside, four reindeer flew around like insects around a porch light. The alfalfa hay he'd set out for them seemed to please their palates. Once their mouths were full, they kicked off the floor and floated around the twelve-foot-by-fifteen-foot room. Two chased each other around the walls, running around like they were in a washing machine.

The sliced carrots in Hannah's hand enticed one reindeer to approach the barred gate between them. His flexible lips explored her hand as his nostrils took in her scent. Finding a carrot slice, it bit into it and flew away. Another soon took its place. The other two crowded around her hand, taking slices before flying off. As she pulled another handful of carrot slices from her bag, she heard the barn door behind her open and close. A familiar touch told her Headless had joined her to see the flying creatures.

"They're cute little things, aren't they," Hannah said as one took a carrot and flew away. "It's amazing how something so small can pull a large sleigh overfilled with toys around the world on a single night."

Taking a carrot slice from her to feed to one hovering in front of him, he remarked, "What's amazing is how he keeps them under control. They seem as chaotic as mosquitoes."

Silence filled the barn, broken only by occasional hoofbeats against the walls or ceiling and the laughter of the observers. The reindeer seemed to enjoy the audience and increased the complexity of their antics. The air movement carried bits of hay upward with it, adding to the mix of fur, antlers, and dust. Some of it made its way up Hannah's nose and she sneezed.

Headless pulled Hannah away from the furry flurry and led her outside the barn. As he secured the door, he commented, "At least they're getting exercise and seem happy. I'll have to scrub the stall out after they leave. The horses may not like their scent."

In the fading light of day, they saw Santa coming across the lawn toward them with Elwin at his side. As he approached, he let out his traditional laugh.

"I have permission from NORAD to go home tonight so we'll be leaving before too long. I'll help Elwin get the reindeer hooked up and check them to make sure they're ready to go."

Relief spread through Hannah like a warm IV. "That's good news. You'll be in your own beds tonight. Sharon will rest better there after her ordeal. But why doesn't she use the talisman? It would be faster."

Even in the dim light, she saw the twinkle in Santa's eyes fade as he said, "She lost it. When she took her shower, she noticed it was gone."

Headless stiffened beside Hannah. "Could it be in our house somewhere? Or in her clothes?"

Shaking his head, Santa replied, "We checked her clothes and everywhere she's been. Essie looked for it with no luck. It must have come off while she was at the cottage. She said she had her hand on it when the clock fell."

"Essie's still here?" Hannah muttered under her breath, hoping no one heard. Sharon was going home, Essie should too. There was no reason for her to hang around any longer. Unless she'd lost her talisman too.

Headless turned to Hannah and bumped her elbow. "This could be a problem. Sharon's magical talisman is out there somewhere. If it's discovered, who knows what could happen."

Visions of the storm swept through Hannah's mind. The rising water, the blowing sand, the roofless cottage. Without the walls to protect it, the storm likely claimed the talisman.

"If it's at the cottage, it's lost forever. Washed out to sea or buried under the sand. I doubt anyone will find it."

Santa shook his head. "She'll be lost without it. It spoiled her, but she'll have to get used to our old ways of travel."

"Even if it's found..." Hannah had to think a minute, but she was sure there was no danger. "It's not much use to anyone unless they know the magic words to get it to work, and I doubt people would guess them."

"You're right," Headless said. "I'll talk to Mrs. Hagg about it. Maybe she can make Sharon another one. But first—" he turned to Santa, "—let's get you ready to go."

Not waiting to hear their plans, Hannah rushed off to the house. Essie was in a corner of the kitchen on the phone with her family. Sharon was propped up in the recliner, eyes closed. Her face was pale, but her cheeks had color in them. Hannah pulled a lap quilt off the sofa and gently spread it across Sharon.

"Thanks." Sharon didn't open her eyes to say it. Her hands fumbled until they found the edge of it and pulled it up higher around her face. "I'm going home today," she mumbled. A tear slid to the smile wrinkles and followed them to her jaw. "In a sleigh."

Pushing an ottoman to the side of the recliner, Hannah took a seat and Sharon's hand. "I'm sorry you got hurt and lost your talisman, but I'm glad Santa is here to take you home. You'll feel better in your house and be back on your feet sooner."

"It's your fault. You should have stayed with me."

Disguised as a boxer's glove, the words hit her square in the gut. A cheap shot from her verbal assailant. Her initial rebuttal was silence, the words stuck behind the lump in her throat.

"Wait. What?" It was all she could manage to say. Even though her sister lay there injured, heat started building inside Hannah. The situation wasn't her fault. "I told you we needed to go. I told you the storm was too bad to wait on Father. I thought you and I agreed. I thought we were leaving together." Not knowing where to release her frustration, she stood and kicked the ottoman back to its regular place. Waiting a minute to see if any word of correction or apology came out of Sharon was a hopeless cause. Every iota of sympathy went out the window.

She had to get out of the room before her tongue released its own retaliatory shot to Sharon's gut. Stomping off to the kitchen only increased the heat inside her. She shot a look at Essie that told her to get off the phone and leave. Her dish cloth was pushed under the faucet and wetted before it was used to wring out every bit of her anger inside her. She wet it again and pictured Sharon's neck as she twisted the cloth tighter and tighter. After every drop was out of the cloth, she spread it out like a lacy handkerchief and leaned over the sink.

Releasing her anger helped her mind and made things perfectly clear. It wasn't her fault Sharon was injured. She'd begged Sharon to leave with her. Sharon said she would. When she snapped home, Sharon was supposed to be right behind her. Other than physically dragging her back, she'd done everything she could do. Sharon's foolishness, waiting for their father to come, caused her injuries. The fault lay with her.

Mumbled voices came from the living room. Essie and Sharon were probably talking about her. If they were ganging up on her, she'd put an end to the slanderous gab session. She started to march out and declare her defiance, but Essie met her at the dining table and pushed her back into the kitchen.

"Sharon told me what she said to you," Essie whispered as she looked back over her shoulder. "I know it hurt your feelings, but let it go. Remember she almost drowned so her memories of the storm are scrambled a little. She doesn't mean anything she says right now."

Hannah crossed her arms and tapped her foot. She couldn't bring herself to admit it, but Essie made sense. Still, the revelation didn't take the sting out of her words or quell the heat burning her insides. A concussion might have made Sharon say what she was feeling inside without any filters. No matter. It was a lie.

"Essie, I begged her to come with me. Before I left, she said she was right behind me." She threw her hands in the air and turned in a tight circle. "I believed her! So I left." She wagged her finger in Essie's face. "I didn't abandon her there. I thought she was coming."

Essie grabbed her finger and pushed it away. "I believe you so quit spitting venom at me." She moved around Hannah and started opening cabinets.

Hannah rolled her eyes. Why didn't she just ask. "The glasses are to the left of the sink." The urge to scream Everybody out! was almost uncontrollable. Her house seemed too full. Too many people were making demands on her. Too many things were disturbing her comfort zone. She needed her routine and homespun peace with only her boys and Headless. Family relationships were fine but in small doses. And at someone else's house.

Clenching her teeth, she took a cleansing breath and tried to dig up inner strength. Santa was hooking up his reindeer in preparation to get Sharon out of the house. There'd be no reason for Essie to stay so she would go. She could stand them a little while longer. It's what her mother would want her to do.

The front door opened, and a voice rang out in surprise. Hannah and Essie rushed to the living room to see Huntley silhouetted in the front doorway and temporarily frozen in place. Horace peeked around him into the room, his backpack falling off his shoulder onto his forearm. With open mouths, their eyes flicked between their aunts and their mother.

Huntley took another step inside, threw his backpack on the floor, and asked, "Having a party without us?"

Rubbing her forehead, Hannah replied, "I thought you were staying late for basketball practice?"

Horace followed his brother in. "Mom, it's seven o'clock. How late did you want us to stay? We're hungry!"

Hannah rubbed her forehead. "Of course, you are. I'll get something for you in a minute." She pointed at the backpacks. "And you have homework to complete."

Ignoring his mother, Horace moved to Sharon and asked what was wrong. She said she'd taken ill and was about to leave to go home.

"In time for you to do your homework," Hannah added.

After the moaning and griping, Huntley asked, "Is Uncle Santa still here? We want to see him and the reindeer." Sharon's nod sent the boys on the run to the barn.

The distraction dissipated the tension in the room. The anger Hannah felt had dropped below the red zone. She couldn't change the past and what happened to Sharon, but she could change what was bound to come up again.

"Look, I didn't desert you, Sharon. I thought you were coming right behind me." Hannah opened her arms to her sisters. "And I moved the money to a bank. There was no evil intent, no greed, no attempt to defraud either of you in my doing so. I did it to keep the money safe and earning interest. If I hadn't, we'd have reason to cry."

Essie and Sharon exchanged glances and shrugs. They grudgingly accepted her excuse but were still suspicious.

Putting the footrest down, Sharon sighed. "You didn't come back for me when I didn't follow you here. You waited a while."

"I thought you were coming. The storm was howling. Any halfway intelligent person would know it was time to leave. I assumed you were—" She stopped herself from saying what she was thinking. The words wouldn't help her peacemaking efforts.

"And you!" Hannah turned to face Essie who looked like she'd been raised on sour pickles. "I will email you the records showing the money in the bank. You'll see that it's all there other than what was paid for upkeep of the cottage."

With raised eyebrows and a sniff, Essie asked, "Do we have access to the money?"

Hannah moved to the sofa, suddenly tired on her feet. The long day full of unexpected events was taking its toll. "Not yet, but I have an idea. Let's see a lawyer and set up a trust fund. A non-negotiable trust fund we three administer. That way if something happens to one of us, the other two can easily take over and ensure the taxes and other expenses are paid."

Essie joined her on the sofa. "I don't know much about them.

"Go on-line and research it. It's a good way to handle the money and a good way to pass it on to our children." Sharon had a pained look on her face. "I'm too tired to think about it."

"Don't worry," Hannah told her, "Essie and I can take care of it. When it's time to sign the papers, we'll make sure you're there."

"No!" Sharon sat up straighter. "You'll not do another thing without me!" Holding her head, she moaned loudly.

Hannah wanted to do the same thing but refrained. "We'll take care of it another time after we know more about how the cottage fared during the storm. If it's gone, this is all moot." Not hearing any argument, she considered the issue put to rest.

Chapter 8

Essie

The day had seemed interminably long. Between the calls from home, Hannah's loud preparation of dinner, and Sharon's constant need for attention, Essie's nerves were threadbare. Nothing had been done about the clock or the money.

Since Sharon and Hannah were unfriendly to each other, it fell to Essie to watch over Sharon. She complained she was getting stiff from sitting and said her muscles protested when she moved. When not complaining about that, she worried and cried over the clock's fate. Her alternating foci of panic kept her restless and crying out her fears. The emotional roller coaster showed no signs of slowing.

The urge to snap home for a little while was overwhelming for Essie, but the secret of the talisman had to be preserved. Hannah's boys thought everyone was going home in the sleigh with Santa. Her leaving early would be suspicious, triggering the intelligent boys to ask too many questions. Once they, or her children, found out about the magical object, they'd each want one for themselves. It would be safer to turn them loose with the keys to the car. The size of the gas tank would limit their range, but with the talisman, they could go anywhere.

Letting out a wail, Sharon cried out, "We've got to go back and get the clock." She grabbed Essie's hand. "Go get Santa. Tell him to take the sleigh to the cottage."

Essie lightly squeezed her hand with all the compassion she could muster. "He's taking you home so you can recover from your near-death ordeal. The storm is still raging there so it's not safe to go. We'll worry about the clock later."

"NO! Santa can get the clock! He can put the clock in, come get me, and take both of us to the North Pole for repairs."

"Not tonight. Maybe—"

A voice from the kitchen came screaming out. "Shut up!" Hannah came into the living room and put her hands on her hips. "Enough about the clock! I'm tired of hearing about it." She bent over Sharon. "I'll go check on the cottage when the storm is past and not a minute sooner. Spare our ears and sit quietly until you can go home." Without another word, she spun on her heels and went back into the kitchen."

After handing a tissue to Sharon to quietly sob into, Essie went to the farthest corner of the living room and sat with her knees drawn as close to her chest as she could get them. Her thirteen children had never pushed her this close to the edge of a screaming fit. The talisman seemed heavy around her neck, beckoning her to use it. With a few words she could use it to return home. Easter had a way of calming her. She needed his strength to regain her ground. Only the matter of the money had kept her here initially, but now, preserving the secrecy of the talisman imprisoned her in this awful place.

Outside the front window, the hellhounds Styx and Shuck played together, chasing a squirrel up a tree. The carefree scene contrasted with the daggers and lightning on her side of the glass. Across the ocean, her children were settled in their beds, most sleeping, a few reading books by flashlights under the covers.

Only by blinking hard could she keep the tears in rather than allowing them to roll freely. She pulled out her cell phone and called Easter. With each ring, she grew more desperate to hear his voice. At the verge of hanging up, his voice came on over the sound of the factory in the background.

"Hello, my love. Risking your life again?"

His tone of voice delivered a soured shot of comfort from her ear to her heart. His voice, although snarky, revived her tattered nerves a little. A smile spread across her face and into her voice. "No, I'm safe. I needed to hear your voice."

"You sound a little tense. What's going on?"

Ignoring Sharon's whimpering, she told him of Hannah's many trips to the cottage without them and of her moving the money to a bank account only she had access to. Of the broken pact between them. Of the building distrust and her growing resentment. She concluded with a heavy sigh.

Easter didn't respond. His silence drove her crazy. He should tell her he understood. He should tell her she was right to feel the way she did. Why would he take so long to say it?

When he did respond, his disappointment came through his voice. "I think Hannah was being smart. If she hadn't moved the money, it might be gone now. I think she deserves a big pat on the back."

What? Had she heard right? Those weren't the words she wanted to hear. Her husband ought to take her side in this, but he wasn't. He probably didn't hear her right. After all, he was a man and didn't always listen well.

"I have every right to be upset. We agreed not to visit the cottage unless all of us could go. And she should have told us what she was doing with the money."

"I've told you before how I feel about it. This so-called pact you three made was dumb, turning the cottage into basically an abandoned building. Deterioration would start, making the place unlivable. Your mother would hate the slow erosion of her cottage."

His logic was killing her resentment of Hannah. He was wadding up her right to feel angry about Hannah's actions and throwing it back in her face.

He continued his campaign. "Tell Hannah thank you for watching the cottage. You haven't done anything to help. Seems to me she deserves the money, unless Sharon helped her. If so, the two of them deserve the money."

"But our kids—"

"Quit using them as a crutch. Our kids are old enough to see after themselves. It's good for them to learn how to do things and support themselves. Any money they have they'll earn just like their grandparents and parents did. Stop letting opportunities pass by while you hide behind them."

She hated when he used the children against her. She'd brought the topic up first. They still needed her, like when they were babies. So what if her triplets were nine years old? Their teenaged siblings didn't do a good job watching them and keeping them out of trouble. When they were grown and gone, she'd have time to do more for him and her sisters. Easter ought to understand her responsibilities to her children. Besides, guilt trips were a mother's forte. His meager attempts at it wouldn't work on her.

"You're not being fair to me."

The sound of tapping fingers came through the call, followed by a yawn. "You were happy when you reconnected with your sisters. Hang on to that feeling. Don't blow it by causing a fuss over money."

His attitude was more than she could handle. His voice had become grating and her last frazzled nerve was unraveling. "Gotta go," she said trying not to say it too tersely. "Hannah has dinner ready. Bye." She hung up without waiting for his response.

She hadn't actually lied to him. The aroma of spaghetti sauce and garlic bread drifted from the kitchen and made her stomach rumble. The sounds of men's voices and laughing boys came from the back porch. The living room would soon fill with people. No sense staying where she was, crumpled up like a discarded newspaper.

Unfolding herself, she arose from her corner seat and stretched. The blood began to circulate in her legs again, making them feel funny. After a quick check on the slumbering Sharon, she headed to the kitchen.

"Easter says thanks for looking after the cottage."

Hannah didn't pause as she drained the pasta into the sink. The pot let out a bang as she put it back on the gas stovetop. "Tell Easter thanks." Going to the cabinet, she pulled out a stack of plates. "Set these around the table." She slid the stack down the countertop toward Essie.

Catching the stack of plates before they tumbled off the countertop to the floor, Essie gritted her teeth. Through the laundry room door came the guys from the barn, pushing the time to discuss their broken pact to later.

Santa went to help Sharon sit up in the recliner.

Quickly setting the table, Essie greeted Headless as he came into the dining room.

He nodded to her and went quickly to his wife's side.

"Wash up," she told him. "Dinner's ready."

He gave her a quick kiss on the top of her head before calling their boys to come wash their hands with him.

"Santa, why don't you fix a plate for Sharon," Hannah called out. "She can eat in the recliner."

The red-shirted, rotund man came in and said, "She's sleeping. She can eat when I get her home. I'm sure Martha will have something prepared for us when we arrive."

The meal went by with the boys and the men doing the conversing. Essie didn't look at Hannah. She didn't want the smoldering embers of anger to flash into flames in front of her nephews. The less they knew of the growing feud, the better, although Huntley seemed to notice something was amiss. He tried to draw his mother and aunt into the conversation and seemed puzzled when they didn't take the bait.

Sharon awoke during the meal and was uncomfortable enough to whine about it. Santa helped her to the table, but she didn't eat. The daggers from her eyes to her sisters conveyed how she felt about them, but she never mentioned it.

Essie figured Sharon felt the same as she did about Hannah's covert activities. They should demand an accounting of their mother's money to make sure it hadn't been spent on the Horseman family or farm. If Hannah ever asked for additional funds, they'd know some sort of embezzling had taken place. The money they found in the cottage was more than enough to take care of expenses. She'd suggested they divide it, but the other two outvoted her.

The boys wandered off to their rooms to do homework. Headless turned on the TV to the weather channel. The backside of the hurricane was making its way across Florida. With the sunrise, the storm would be over, and the first photos of the damages would come. The news report answered her questions.

They went out to the patio and watched as Elwin, Sharon, and Santa flew away in the sleigh. As they stood there, Essie waited and wondered. She knew she was expected to leave too, but what about the cottage? Was there a plan or would Hannah keep it a secret too?

Turning to her, Hannah asked, "Why are you still here?"

The first arrow had landed on target. The fatigue of the long day was setting in, making her wave the white flag. "What do you want to do with the cottage now? Do you need help checking it?"

As Hannah took her defiant stance, Headless put himself between her and her sister. Even Essie could read the telepathy passing between them. He mentally told Hannah to take it easy.

A hand through her hair and a deep breath seemed to restore her control. "Yes, I could use the help," Hannah said in a voice freezing in the air between them.

"Fine. When?"

Tapping her foot, Hannah looked everywhere around the yard except at her sister. "Day after tomorrow. Come back, and we'll go together."

"Santa's coming back?"

The voice behind her made Essie spin around. Horace stood at the back door, eavesdropping on the adults. The innocence of the question showed in his eyes.

Headless went to tend his offspring. "I thought you were doing your homework, son."

"I'm done, Dad. If Aunt Essie is going home and coming back the day after tomorrow, Santa has to take her, right? Did he leave a reindeer for her?" He took a step toward Essie. "Can I ride along? Aunt Essie, can I spend the night with you?"

Words eluded Essie. What was the proper response? She hoped for an answer in Hannah's face, but found nothing but the fear of discovery of their secret.

Huntley came outside, his head cocked and a sly look on his face. "It's interesting how Sharon and Santa have gone home, but you haven't, Aunt Essie. Want to tell us how you get between places so fast if you don't use the reindeer?" At the edge of the patio, he crossed his arms like a parent who caught a child sneaking a cookie.

A blink of the eyes was the only sign of life before Hannah said, "How long have you been listening to us?"

Huntley wagged his shoulders. "Long enough to know Santa ain't coming back for Aunt Essie. You and she have a sort of magic that lets you go back and forth without him." Wiggling eyebrows emphasized his smug look.

Hannah bit her bottom lip and poked a finger at him. "You're in trouble. You know better than to eavesdrop."

"Oh, Mom," Huntley came into the living room. "How did you think you could keep it hidden from us? We're not dumb you know. Your beach towel and bathing suit drying in the laundry room. Your tan. You've been visiting Grandma's beach house while we were at school."

Headless chuckled as he put his hand over his mouth. "Told you," he said softly.

Hannah's face turned red. Her shoulders drooped as she hugged her midsection.

Huntley added. "So what? It's only for grownups?"

From the look on Huntley's face, Essie knew this was about to escalate. This was no place for her. "If you'll excuse me, I think I'll go home," she told the family before going into the house and into the bathroom. Quickly she whispered the chant to her talisman and got out of there before the fireworks began.

Chapter 9

Sharon

A cool front headed south from the Arctic bounced the sleigh around when it went over the U.S. border. Sharon groaned as her head pounded with each bump. Santa reassured her they would be home soon. She snuggled deeper into the warm woolen blankets. The top of her head stuck out, her short hair rippling and twisting in the air as they went over the snow-covered ground of northern Canada.

Sharon longed for the embrace of her bed and its warmth beneath the layers of blankets. She'd feel better and could deal with her unsettled feelings about Hannah. She'd deceived them and their pact. She'd spent time at the cottage, alone, without her or Essie having a chance to approve or disapprove. She'd moved the money out of its hiding place into a bank account. What else might she have done secretly? Essie had been so hostile to her and Hannah. From the way she acted, it was like a guilty conscious was making her unfriendly. What did Essie know or do without telling her and Hannah?

Never in the past had Sharon distrusted her family so much.

A knot formed in her stomach, making her ribs hurt, as she thought about the clock. It was likely damaged—or, heaven forbid, destroyed—by the storm. How could it not be? After the roof blew off, nothing could have saved it other than her father, and he hadn't come.

The clock was more than an inanimate object. Its magic powers made it alive. Her mother lived in it. Her father was connected to it. It could alter time. The loss of the clock was more than losing a piece of furniture; it was losing a piece of her heart. Despite that, a part of her was glad it was destroyed. When it fell on her, it held her head underwater, attempting to drown her. The clock was like a murderer, taking revenge on her for not protecting it from the water. Or maybe it was tired of waiting on Essie to come take her turn at calling their mother. Or maybe it was tired of being idle. Maybe it was angry about being alone. Maybe it was best to leave it buried in the sand.

Yet, the clock held her connection to their father so it had to be repaired. Sea water with its salt content had probably damaged the inner workings. The wooden case would be warped and moldy and need to be replaced. It seemed logical that whatever made the clock magical wasn't part of the woodworking. The magic had to come from the inner workings and how the gears worked together. The elves who were metallurgists could help them repair the metal parts of the clock and the engineers could help them put it back together. The woodworkers could make a new case. But would it be enough to bring the magic back?

The sleigh made a slight bump as they landed. Sharon pushed the blanket back and saw golden lights shining out of the windows of her home at the North Pole. The door opened, and Martha and Elwina came rushing out to greet the couple. Santa and Martha helped Sharon from the sleigh as Elwin tended to the reindeer. Elwina held the front door wide as they went inside the cozy, warm house.

"Straight to bed with you," Elwina said as she guided Sharon down the hallway.

Too tired to be polite, Sharon refused the help. "I'm not an invalid. I bruised some things, that's all."

Elwina shushed her. "We heard you almost drowned. We must take care it doesn't turn into pneumonia."

Martha rushed into the bedroom and pulled back the covers on the large bed. As she fluffed the pillows and arranged them, she said, "I've got nice, warm soup ready for you. It's my special blend. It'll help you feel better in no time." The two elves rushed off to the kitchen.

After her friends left, Sharon changed into her night clothes while fighting off the dizziness from walking so far and settled into her soft comfy bed. The attention was unnecessary. She wasn't sick but grieving. She'd lost her parents and her talisman. Time would pass slowly while she tried to get over the losses.

Relief bubbled up through her black mood as she reminded herself that her dream hadn't come true. Essie was alive and safe at home with her family. The soup might help but being in her home and in her bed had already made her feel better. Her head quit pounding and her ribs quit aching as she lay there. If Santa gave her a foot rub, her recovery would be kickstarted.

As if reading her mind, Santa appeared. He sat on the edge of the bed and let out a soft chuckle. "I thought a foot rub might help you, but I can tell you're already feeling relaxed."

A sigh of contentment was her only answer to him.

The sound of a rolling cart came from the hallway, followed shortly by the real thing appearing in the open bedroom door. It was loaded with a soup tureen, bowls, plates of bread and cheese, and steaming cups of tea. Elwina put a bed table across Sharon's lap, and Martha began to set her little table.

Santa rose and excused himself. "The workshop needs my attention. I think your nurses will take excellent care of you, my dear." He gave the ladies a smile and a wink as he left.

The warm aroma of beef, carrots, and potatoes rose to meet her nose. Her stomach rumbled its request for a serving or two. The first spoonful tickled her taste buds and slid down her throat like molasses out of a jar. Beef stew had never tasted so good.

Martha climbed onto the foot of the bed. "Tell us what happened."

Elwina crawled up beside Martha. "We heard you almost died! Oh dear! I can't even think of it!" She dabbed her eyes with the edge of her apron.

The stew warmed Sharon's throat and insides all the way to her soul. The balminess of the liquid and her friends' friendship revived her like nothing else had done. She forgot about her aches and pains and basked in the comfort of her home. She took another spoon of stew and reveled in the flavor before telling them the story of her adventure while eating her supper.

"Great balls of tinsel!" Martha uttered when Sharon talked about the clock falling on her. "We're lucky you're still with us." She patted her heart like she would a baby's back.

Taking the bed table away, Elwina said, "We should let you rest. You'll feel more like yourself after a good night's sleep." Martha made sure Sharon was tucked in as Elwina rolled the cart away.

It was still light outside, but Sharon was somewhere in the depths of dreamland. She was in her mother's cottage. Everything was tidy and in its place. The clock stood against the wall showing nine-fifteen. The leather sofa and overstuffed chair were positioned for watching the large TV and the videos from the closet. The money was in its hiding place. The kitchen was full of baking ingredients and the scent of her mother's cooking. She was safe and happy at the cottage. Her father stood in front of her, smiling like he always did when he was pleased with her.

But something wasn't right. The clock drew her to it, now reading ten o'clock. Thinking hard about it, she was sure it had never been that time before. The pendulum glinted in the light as it swung back and forth. Reaching out, she felt the polished wood of the clock under her hand. Her chest felt tight, and she was getting hotter. Something deep down told her she needed to do something, but she didn't know what. She turned to ask her father if he knew. Her jaw moved, but no words came from her mouth.

Still her father seemed to know what she was thinking. "You need to come together with your sisters." His eyes were intense, staring at her, trying to convey his thoughts. "Come together with your sisters."

She reached out to touch him, but her hand never reached him. Between them seemed to be a chasm through the living room. He couldn't cross and neither could she. So close yet so far, she tried to voice the words on her tongue, but nothing came.

"Come together with your sisters."

The words didn't make sense. She tried to ask him why but still couldn't get the words to come out.

"Come together with your sisters."

He continued to say the words over and over, faster and faster as his figure began to fade. She wanted him to stay and reached her arms wide to invite him over the divide. But the chasm grew wider. Fear, confusion, and desperation interfused as the features of the living room began to fade as well. Questions needed to be asked and answered. She didn't want it to end. She fell to the floor and tried to hold it back. Memories of wind and water took over the scene, bringing fear with it.

Blackness engulfed her. Crying out, she sat up in bed with such a start her ribs and head ached. Where was she?

She rubbed her eyes and looked around. She was in her bedroom. In her home. At the North Pole. But she'd been in her mother's cottage only an instant ago. Feeling around her neck for her father's necklace, she found it there, warmed by her skin. Slowly, she lay back on the pillows and pulled the comforter up around her. Had it been a dream? Her memory of being at the cottage was so vivid. She must have been there. It felt like she'd actually lived it.

Her breath came quickly, and the room started to spin. Was it only a dream? Or was it a premonition? What was real and what was not? What if she were crazy and needed to be locked away? What if she died right now? What if— her heart was pounding. Its noise was so loud she couldn't hear anything else. Only the aches seemed real. Everything else was confusion.

The door swung open and Santa came running in. "I heard you cry out. What's wrong, sweetheart? Having another panic attack?" He stroked her forehead softly, pushing the hair out of her eyes. He reached into the bed table and pulled out a paper bag. "Breathe into this. It'll help."

Quickly opening the bag, she put it over her mouth and nose and breathed into it. In and out the bag crinkled and wrinkled as panic gripped her. Slowly the speed of its movement slowed, and her head cleared.

"What brought this on?" His voice was smooth as silk, and it comforted her. Like the smell of marshmallows melting in hot chocolate, a sweetness floated in his words. Whenever she was lost in confusion, he knew the answers.

The bag served its purpose, leaving her able to think more clearly. "Was I here all night, or did I snap off to the cottage?"

Santa's eyes widened as did his mouth. "Were you where? No, my dear. You were here through the whole night. I checked on you several times. Besides…" he sat on the side of the bed "…you lost your talisman. Remember? You couldn't have gone to the cottage without it."

She rubbed her forehead. It slowly came back to her. "I remember now. Is the cottage still there? Is it okay? I need my talisman. I have to go back. The clock. I have to save the clock."

"There's no need to go." He stared at his hands. "Hannah and Essie will take care of it and let you know." He cleared his throat. "I'm sorry to tell you this, but according to the news reports, the hurricane pretty much wiped out all the houses close to the beaches. From the videos I've seen, I doubt anything is still there."

"And the clock?"

"It's gone."

"No! I saw it. I touched it."

He stared into her eyes and shook his head.

Looking away, the confusion vanished, and she understood. She was either crazy or it was a dream. She'd hang onto the least worrisome. "It must have been a dream. But it was a very REAL dream."

"Tell me about it."

The dream was easy to recall, like remembering what happened a minute ago. "I was in the cottage with Father. He kept telling me 'Come together with your sisters.' He said it over and over again."

"What do you think it means?"

Her father's wish was a futile one. Essie had her busy life and little interest in keeping touch with her sisters. Hannah had broken their pact and acted in her best interest instead of the three of them. With the cottage and the clock gone, there was nothing left to hold them together. Even the videos were gone. Coming together with those two, as their father had instructed her, seemed less and less possible. It was moving toward impossible and improbable.

But the words of her father kept echoing through her head. He told her to come together with them. They had to come together. Disobedience of her father's wishes wasn't acceptable.

"It means I have to find a way to bring us together. It'll be hard, but Father said to. We have to obey him. He'll have the answers for us on what to do. He can help us with the clock. We have to find a way to call him."

Santa brushed her hair back from her face. "He'll know what to do."

Chapter 10

Hannah

Cleaning the kitchen had rarely been so pleasurable. Her company was gone at last. Headless was overseeing Huntley and Horace as they cleaned out the stables in punishment for eavesdropping. The chore had to be completed before they could participate in their normal Saturday activities. The house belonged to Hannah and her alone. Peace and quiet settled over the house again.

In their twenty years of marriage, she and Headless rarely hosted guests for dinner, much less overnight. Occasionally, the boys had friends over, but those times involved baking frozen pizzas, popping popcorn, and providing other unhealthy snacks. Having her sisters unexpectedly snap in and stay longer than expected had caused too much stress. She didn't mind meeting her sisters at her mother's cottage but having them invade her personal space—her haven—was more than she could handle.

Sharon's barbed words still stung where they'd hit. While true she'd snapped back without bringing Sharon with her, she'd truly thought Sharon was right behind her. Still, she should have known she'd hang back. Sharon's obsession with the clock in the middle of the hurricane seemed crazy at the time. Her staying to save it was crazier. Self-preservation should have been her first worry, not the clock.

Wringing the dishcloth with the strength of aggravation, nearly every drop of water came out. She wiped it along the granite countertops, pushing the few crumbs into her hand and depositing them into the sink.

If Headless hadn't been able to get to the cottage, Sharon might have drowned under the clock. He became an instant hero, and she became the dunce for having allegedly left Sharon. That compounded her ire, forcing her into an unusual and uncomfortable place. It wasn't her fault Sharon made a dumb choice.

The back door squeaked its announcement someone was coming in. The person washed their hands in the laundry room sink before coming up behind her. Long arms surrounded her and pulled her close.

"We have a problem," Headless whispered in her ear.

His breath tickled her ear, making her giggle and snuggle farther back into his arms. "Another one? Now what?" she whispered back.

He kissed the back of her neck, sending tingles crawling and squirming over her.

"The boys want talismans for themselves."

The tingles vanished like ice in boiling water. She spun around to face him. "They can't have them. We'd never know where they were."

"Agreed, but they are working up a plan to get one. It involves sweet talking Mrs. Hagg, among other briberies."

She tilted her head. "Were you eavesdropping?"

He winked at her. "Parents are allowed to eavesdrop. It's our parental prerogative."

She returned his sly look before turning away to continue wiping the countertops. "I'll talk to Mrs. Hagg first. She'll understand how we feel."

A soft snap came from the living room. A soft groan came from Hannah as Headless let go of her and stepped back. Tossing the dish cloth to him, she went to greet Essie.

The sight stopped her in her tracks. Stoop-shouldered and bleary-eyed, Essie gave a weak smile and waved. "I'm here," she said with faked enthusiasm. Her baggy work pants and faded sweatshirt made her look like a homeless bag lady without the grocery cart.

"You look—" Hannah didn't know what word to use other than awful, but not wanting to upset her sister more than she had to, she chose something truthful but less harsh. "You look tired."

Essie gave a crooked smile. "I haven't slept much the past couple of nights." She rubbed one eye. "The only thing keeping me upright is coffee."

Hannah hadn't slept well either, but after a moment's consideration, she realized she never thought about the time difference between their two homes and how thirteen children would disrupt rest time like a newborn. She could understand why Essie looked like she did. No matter. They needed to check the cottage during the daylight since the power was out in the area. Plus, she needed to be back before her boys went to see Mrs. Hagg. That was paramount. Her dear friend's soft heart was no match against two conniving teenaged boys.

Essie yawned and asked, "Any news from Florida and how bad the damage is?"

Headless came into the room, took the remote, and turned on the TV. Pictures of debris and destroyed houses flashed onto the screen. The reporter went on about the billions of dollars in damage along the coast from the winds and storm surge. The most damage was on the coast but flooding and winds also took its toll farther inland. The videos showed nothing but a tangled mass of splintered wood, sand drifts, and wires covering the ground where residences used to be. Only a few structures were recognizable as houses and buildings. The rest were flattened. What trees were left standing were stripped bare of any foliage. The carnage of nature's war zone.

The sight left Hannah numb inside. The last thread of hope unraveled and fell away. Her secret retreat was gone.

"Maybe Mother's cottage survived," Essie whispered. "It's stone so it's sturdier than stick-built houses."

"I don't see how," Hannah replied as she stared at the TV. "The storm was too intense for anything to remain behind." She looked at Headless who offered nothing but a compassionate stare. She turned back to Essie. "Should we go see?"

Essie's tired face paled a little, but she nodded as she pulled her talisman from under her shirt. "As ready as I'll ever be. Should we take anything along?"

Waving her cell phone in the air, Hannah replied, "Just something to take photos for the insurance company. Let's assess the damage and come back here to decide what we need and how to proceed."

"You two be careful," Headless said as he gave Hannah a peck on the cheek. His head bobbled a little, but he set it still again. "With all the debris around, it will be dangerous to poke around too much. Turn off the gas first thing and watch for electric lines. You never know when they'll fire them back up again."

Hannah's heart skipped a beat. The hazards after the storm hadn't entered her thinking. Good thing Headless brought it to their attention. "We'll be very careful, honey. This is a damage assessment trip. It shouldn't take long to see how bad it is. If nothing is there, our decisions will be easy. If anything is left, we'll figure out what it will take to fix the place after we get back. We should be back before the boys finish their sentence."

A puzzled look crossed Essie's face but was quickly replaced by a knowing nod and a crooked smile.

Hannah held her talisman and nodded at Essie. Both uttered the chant simultaneously.

The familiar swirling and squeezing surrounded Hannah as she transported to her mother's living room by the beach. Her feet gently settled into sand instead of onto the familiar hardwood. Opening her eyes, she didn't recognize where she was. Nothing was familiar. The gentle curve of her beach was gone. The ocean waves lapped at an unfamiliar landscape. The talisman must have made a mistake. They had landed on another beach in front of another cottage.

Essie's pale, open-mouth face stared at something behind her. Turning, the sight sickened her too and caused her stomach to turn to lead. The stone fireplace and part of the wall beside it stood out of the sand. Unnaturally shaped piles of sand marked where the cottage's walls had collapsed and been buried.

Sobs leaked out of Essie and into the air. Hannah couldn't fight off the grief tearing through her, and she joined her sister in grieving the loss. The storm had obliterated the physical icon of their memories. Nothing remained of their childhood home but sand-covered rubble and a makeshift headstone to mark the place where her family once lived and loved.

Hannah wiped away her tears and walked around. In the distance, the neighbors' houses were gone. The house where they'd gone to persuade Captain Fremont to come home was erased from the earth. Did his lighthouse survive the storm? No matter. First things first.

"It's gone!" Essie wailed. She fell to her knees and dug in the sand. "All of it. Even the clock."

Hannah stopped in her tracks. The clock! She fell to her knees beside Essie and took hold of Essie's shoulders. "It was on the floor the last time anyone saw it, right?"

Essie nodded.

Hannah started digging in the sand. "Maybe it's still here. It was too heavy for the water to wash away."

Crawling, they pushed away the dry and wet sand only to have more of it slide in its place. Their efforts seemed futile, but the drive to find the clock propelled them on. Hannah moved away from Essie. The waves that knocked the walls down might have moved the clock toward the back of the house. She dug deeper, moving the sand back farther and farther until the hole was about a yard wide and an arm's length deep. She crawled into the middle of the hole and dug a seat in the side. The perch made her digging labors more comfortable.

Adjusting her position, she felt something poking her backside. Moving herself and a handful of dirt uncovered a leg from the coffee table. She used it like a pick and bulldozer to loosen and push sand away. In one swipe, she hit something that made a funny sound. Digging with her hands uncovered a videotape sticking out of the side of her pit. The heavy weight of it meant it was filled with wet sand. Essie lamented, but nothing could be done to salvage their recorded memories. Rather than dwell on it, the sisters continued their search.

After pushing a larger and larger pile of sand, their digging revealed a sandy, but recognizable hardwood floor.

"We found the floor!" Essie cried out.

The sight brought hope that more might be found. Together they pushed more sand, uncovering more of the floor in the hole they'd dug. As the hole grew wider and deeper, another videotape appeared, then another.

112

Essie held them to her chest like they were made of gold. "This might be Mother's last tape to us."

Hannah shook her head. "It doesn't have our mark on it so it's not. How could it survive with so much sand inside it? They've been ruined so they're useless. Let's use them to dig away more sand. The important thing is finding the clock."

Essie held the tape behind her. "No! I won't let you destroy these last things we have of Mother!"

Hannah waved her hand in the air and held an inner debate on whether to fight her for the additional tool or to let her have it. Choosing not to engage in the battle and expend energy unnecessarily, she cried out, "Whatever! Put it aside and keep digging." She moved away from her sister lest the desire to wrestle the tapes away from Essie became too strong to resist.

The two women dug, paying no attention to the time or anything around them. The sound of the ever-present surf provided them with white noise, occasionally broken by a far-off backup alarm. The smell of seaweed and rotting fish was strong.

Ignoring the sights, sounds, and odors, Hannah continued to move the mounds of sand washed over the cottage by the storm. Her hands were getting tender with the sandpaper effect on her skin. Wood debris mixed in the sand threatened them with splinters and cuts. Bringing gloves along would've been a great idea, but she didn't think they would do anything other than look around. Desperation for the clock had made them go beyond their previous plans.

After what seemed like hours, Hannah's hand hit something under the sand. The promise of uncovering another memento of home made her dig harder with the table leg. In the final few inches, she dug with her hands, brushing

113

sand away until she could see wooden boards stacked on top of one another. To the side of the boards lay a carved piece of wood. It was the top of the grandfather clock. Screaming out her discovery brought Essie over to help her. Together they extended the hole and dug out the remains of the top of the clock. It was face down on the floor, crushed flat like it was a box ready for recycling.

The sisters worked, pushing the sand away. Their excavation was surrounded by mounds so big and deep the sides kept sluffing back into their excavation, making them do double the work. Hannah took the time to move the mounds back away from the clock debris, and progress went faster.

At last the sisters stood above the remains of the destroyed clock. Essie sniffled. "Mother's gone." She wiped her face with her sleeve. "Father's gone. Everything is gone."

The words sunk in on Hannah's head, pushing her heart into her feet and her knees to the ground. The magic clock lay under a heap of wood and splinters, under which she hoped the clock workings and face still lay. Using the coffee table leg, she pried the top boards to the side. Sand was packed underneath them, but parts of gold and metal gears shimmered in the sunlight, taunting her for failing to rescue them from the storm.

Working together, they pushed aside more boards and sand until they could see the workings and back of the clock face. She gingerly cleared sand away from the heart of the clock. Looking for screws or bolts holding everything in place, she loosened them and brushed sand away to free the workings from its wooden coffin. With no screwdriver, the sisters used their fingernails and broken shells to untighten what they could. Unscrewing one last screw, the handless clock face came loose. She lifted it up and cleared the last of the sand sticking to it. Handing it to a sniffing Essie, she dug deeper to find the clock hands. The clock face was nothing without the hour and minute hands.

Essie knelt beside her. "We got what we need with the insides of the clock. Let's go back."

Shaking her head, Hannah kept digging. "How do you know? Maybe it's not the face of the clock that holds the magic. Maybe it's the hands. Or maybe it's the gears."

"We really don't know how this thing works." Essie held the clock face up higher, moving it so its face glinted the sunlight like a mirror. "I hope the elves in Santa's workshop can put it back together again."

They set the loose parts of the clock on the exposed wood floor. They hadn't exposed the pendulum and couldn't free the rest of the workings until they did. The more she thought about it, the more Hannah knew Essie might be right. The magic probably wasn't in the wood case, but in the mechanical parts of the clock. Those pieces and the pendulum could be remounted in a new case. Once repaired, it might work again.

As Hannah brushed the sand away, she said, "Let's leave the wood parts. We can take the metal parts to Santa and see if he and his elves can put it back together."

Agreeing, Essie brushed more sand away as Hannah gingerly pulled and tugged on the casing holding the gears and springs. It moved slightly, and the sisters dug until the works moved.

Hannah pulled a little harder. "The pendulum may be keeping it anchored. We need to disconnect it. Take the table leg and pry the boards up. I'll try to pull the pendulum out."

Repositioning themselves, they put the plan of action into play. In a few minutes, the pendulum slid out from under the boards like a tail on the casing. Its gold patina gleamed in the sunlight like a mirror as they set it on top of the boards formerly housing it.

"Can you believe it?" Essie said, slightly panting from the exertion. She ran her hand across the clock face. "We found the clock! Sharon will be so excited."

Hannah lay back against the sides of the hole. "That's all we need from here. Sharon will be relieved. Let's take it straight to Santa's workshop so they can get to work on it right away. We'll hope the magic will still be there." As she moved to get up, she felt a rock under her foot. She pushed it aside so get a better footing, but something inside her made her look at what had caught her attention. Reaching down, she pulled up a stone with a broken cord tied to it. It swung in the breeze as she held it up.

Essie let out a gasp. "You found Sharon's talisman!"

Hannah couldn't believe her eyes. In the tons of sand, the talisman had turned up as if it wanted to be found. "I can't believe it! It must have broken when the clock fell on her. The clock sheltered it from being washed away. How amazing is that!"

"Freeze!"

A masculine voice behind the barrel of a gun startled her so much she almost dropped the talisman. Hannah did what the word described. Beside her, Essie clutched the clock face to her chest and muttered something.

Two police officers had their revolvers pointed at the sisters. "Put your hands where we can see them!"

Chapter 11

Essie

Essie's heart pounded so loudly it drowned out any sounds attempting to reach her ears. The last thing she'd heard was the voice of authority telling her to freeze. Petrified with fear, she had no problem with complying with order. Except for her lips. Words spilled out and she couldn't stop them. "Oh dear oh dear oh dear…"

"Stand up!" The revolver left no room for argument.

Fear was overwhelming her, and her eyes started to dry out from lack of blinking. She had no identification. Her passport was at home in Germany. Without those, she couldn't prove who she was. She'd seen the news. Undocumented visitors were frowned upon. Defying orders, her hand went to her talisman and the chant threatened to spill off her lips. She couldn't desert Hannah here in front of law enforcement officers. They'd know about the talisman. Rather than go, she'd follow her sister's lead.

Essie moved her eyes so she could see Hannah. Anger covered her sister's face which deepened her fear. She'd seen Hannah's tantrums, none of which ended in a good way. If these guys were policemen, resisting wouldn't accomplish anything. She tried to use telekinesis to send her thoughts over to Hannah. Keep your mouth shut! It didn't work.

"Sir, we have every right to be here! We're taxpayers…"

Essie shut her eyes to block out what followed and waited for the sound of a gun. Hearing them shoot Hannah would make her faint. She hoped they'd shoot her while she was unconscious because she couldn't bear to see the gun fire at her. To keep herself calm, she visualized her family safe and sound and studying in school.

The surf didn't block out the squeaking of the leather belt of the officer behind her. His tone made her pretty sure his gun was still on her. Her heart almost stopped, wondering if a bullet would kill her. An overwhelming terror gripped her heart and squeezed so hard she could hardly stand it. Unable to comply any longer, her legs wobbled, and she fell to the sand.

"Look what you've done to my sister!" Hannah shrieked as she knelt beside Essie. Leaning over, she whispered, "Quit acting like Sharon! Get up!"

"Ma'am, you appear to be rooting through the remnants of this house and stealing valuables. This area is closed to protect it from looters like you. You're under arrest for being in a closed area and being in possession of stolen items. You'll have to come with us."

With eyes still tightly closed, Essie moved with the tugging on her arm. The fear permeating her every pore made it impossible to rise. She was a foreigner, had no passport with her, and came to the country without going through customs or any other security system. No record of her entry made her an undocumented alien. If the police found this out, she'd be thrown into the deepest, darkest dungeon they had, never to be released. She'd never see her family again.

With Hannah pulling harder and hurting her arms, Essie rose to her feet. Sand ran down her legs and into her sand-filled shoes. She held her arms out. "Take me to jail."

Hannah pushed her arms back and yelled, "Are you crazy? This is our cottage. We're going through our stuff. They have nothing to arrest us for."

"Ma'am, this area is closed. You're trespassing whether you own this property or not."

"I—we didn't know, officer," Essie said in her most humble voice.

"That's a lousy excuse. How could you not know?" the other officer asked. "There are signs and tape around the perimeter saying it's off limits to everyone."

Hannah pushed Essie behind her. "We came along the beach and missed it. Look, keep the clock, officers. We'll be happy to vacate the closed area and be on our way." With a short footstep, she went backwards.

This wouldn't do. She whispered out of the side of her mouth, "Hannah, what are you doing?" Giving the officers her best innocent look, she said, "We need the clock. It's of no use to anyone else. Everything else can stay."

"You're not taking anything with you," the man said. "And you're not going anywhere except with us."

Embarrassment pushed Essie's head to her chest. They were caught red-handed. Accused as thieves and looters. Her children would be ashamed of her. They wouldn't visit her in jail. No, she couldn't let this happen. Her children still needed their mother. She had to get out of here. Her hand went to her throat where the leather band held the talisman around her neck. A little chant and she'd be home in no time. She closed her eyes and took a breath.

Another hand tried to pull her hand away from the talisman, but she resisted. Looking out of the side of her eyes, she saw Hannah glaring at her. She got the message. She didn't dare run. Her hand moved away from the hope of deliverance.

One officer walked closer to where they had been digging and pointed. "Been prospecting for gold? Looks like you found the mother lode."

"No!" Hannah put her hands on her hips. "It's not gold. It's our mother's grandfather clock." She pulled her pockets inside out. "See. Nothing else. We want our clock. It's our most precious heirloom. Everything else here can go to the devil as far we're concerned."

The other officer drew closer, his hand on his gun, which sent Essie into a panic. She'd read the American news about how many gun deaths there were. She needed to go home to her children but not with a gunshot wound. How would she explain it? Her kids would freak.

The taller man took a step toward them. His camouflage uniform had two stripes on the arm. "What's that thing in your hand? A key?"

Hannah's hand went behind her back. "Nothing."

He held out his hand and wagged his fingers with a give-me motion.

Cooperating on her own terms, Hannah held the talisman by the cord and let it swing in front of her. "It's a stone on a string. It broke while we were digging. See, my sister and I have one like it." She elbowed Essie. They pulled out their talismans to show.

The man repeated the motion.

Essie made a grab for Sharon's talisman but missed it when Hannah pulled it close to her chest. "This," Hannah said, "is a valued and significant family heirloom too. We can't give it to you. It's got no value to anyone but us."

One of the officers stepped behind them, and the man in front took a step closer. "You can make this easy or you can make it hard. Give the alleged heirloom to me. We're taking you to base and if and when you prove you're not looters, you'll get the necklace back." He held his arm out and wagged his fingers at her.

With Sharon's talisman in her fist, Hannah gave Essie a quick questioning look.

Essie nodded slightly. They were in enough trouble without disobeying the order.

"Fine," Hannah spat out as she slapped the talisman in the outstretched hand.

Essie's heart was racing so fast she thought it would explode. The situation was untenable. Jail time as an undocumented invader would last the rest of her life—or at least until her kids were all in or out of college. If she was deported, she'd have to go through so much red tape it would be like untangling fishing line. She'd never get back home. Her children would be ashamed of her. Easter would—well, who knew what he'd do to her. Take her talisman and never give it back.

Her passport. That's what she needed. Although it wasn't stamped showing legal entry to the country, it would prove her identity and might be enough to keep her out of jail. She needed to go home, but to leave Hannah in this distressful situation would be unforgivable. If only there were another way—

She stepped out from behind Hannah. "Please ask the Sarasota County Sheriff's officers if they know us. They helped us when we were here a few years ago. Officers Stanus and---and—"

"Officer Hanover," Hannah added with a bright look at Essie. "They'll vouch for us. Just ask them. They know who we are." She turned her face toward Essie and whispered, "I hope they remember us."

One man motioned for them to start walking. "Don't worry. We'll be turning you over to them for prosecution.

C'mon. Let's go back to our checkpoint." He continued to wave toward the other man who started walking backwards, never letting his eyes off them.

Essie's heart froze, petrifying her again. They were going to jail. She looked at her feet where the clock face lay in the sand. She quickly dropped to her knees and pushed it back into the sand and covered it with more. Hannah dropped beside her and helped her.

"What are you doing?"

The men came to the edge of their excavation. The sisters pushed sand over the clock face and workings. Neither officer interfered as they pushed the piles of sand back into the hole and smoothed it off.

Essie rose to her feet and spoke with false confidence. "If we're going with you, we want to hide this so no looters get it. The clock belongs to us. It's ours because this is—was our cottage."

"Prove it," one man said, his tone implying impatience. "Let's see an ID. If this really is your place, your driver's license will have this address."

The blood grew cold in Essie. How could she explain she'd entered the country illegally, but not exactly? They would deport her after going through court or some other drawn out process. She shook her head, trying to push the guilt and stress away. "This is the cottage our mother left to us. Go look it up in the records."

"Doesn't matter. If you don't show us your ID here, they'll ask for it at the checkpoint."

Hannah stepped forward. "We lost it. While we were getting here, it must have fallen out of my pocket."

The man turned toward Essie. "And your story?"

"Same as hers." It was the best she could come up with even though she knew it was a lame excuse. Her brain was too full of visions of iron bars and concrete floors to come up with something better.

The older man said, "Doesn't explain why you're here when this area is closed to everyone, including homeowners. You have to come with us." Again, the man motioned for them to come along with them

Hannah hooked her arms in Essie's. "Don't worry, sis. Once Hanover and Stanus see us, they'll explain everything. This is our house, and we have every right to be here. They were there more than once."

One officer grumped as he walked alongside them. "You cause a lot of trouble in your neighborhood?" He walked over to his partner. "We need to cuff these two in case they try something."

Essie's pulse skyrocketed. They were doomed. She couldn't run home to get her passport while handcuffed to Hannah. If she was going to do something, it had to be now. Hannah was busy explaining why Stanus and Hanover had visited the cottage. One officer was listening to Hannah and the other was calling in to the checkpoint with the radio, checking on what to do. She grabbed her talisman and whispered,

"PopmybubbleI'mintroubletakemethereonthedouble. Hometakemehome!"

Chapter 12

Sharon

Sharon's kitchen buzzed with activity as Martha Elf and her daughters fixed sandwiches for the workers in the toy factory. Relegated to only watching, Sharon sat pouting in the corner. Martha insisted she needed rest for her two-day-old bruises. According to Clarina, their medical nurse at the workshop, these bruises and the trauma of the event warranted rest.

Sharon let out an unhappy snort. Rest wouldn't cure what was really wrong with her. The clock was to blame for her misery. She tried to save it, but it turned on her, assaulted her as it fell on top of her. Her aches and bruises were a constant reminder of the attack. Her parents were gone for sure now. All because of the stupid, heavy clock. Why didn't her father give her mother a mantel clock? Or a wristwatch? That would have been easy to save. She'd have made it back to Hannah's house unbruised and victorious.

One of the girls offered Sharon a sandwich, but she waved it away. Her knotted stomach wouldn't welcome anything right now. She pulled her cell phone out of her pocket and checked it for the umpteenth time since she sat. Still no word from her sisters on the condition of the cottage. Her stomach knotted tighter. Had they forgotten about her? What if they were glad she was out of the equation? They were free to do whatever they wanted without her dissenting voice.

Or maybe they were tired of dealing with her panic attacks. Sharon slumped in her seat. She was too. She was tired of the paper bags, the pounding heart, the fear gripping her like a vise. She'd put up with it by assuming it was her cross to bear. But lately, Clarina told her there were herbal medicines to help her with the attacks. She'd brushed them aside previously, but it was time to reconsider.

The chattering of Martha and the girls grated on her nerves. Never one to sit still while others worked, she left the kitchen. What was once her haven and place of therapy had been colonized by the capable hands of others.

Her whole body felt like it was made of lead. Dragging herself to the bedroom took more effort than she wanted to expend. Once she got there, she flung herself face-down on the bed. Breathing into her comforter quelled her anxiety better than a paper bag.

Time drifted by like the snowflakes going past the window. The snows of depression grew deeper, burying her as she lay unmoving.

A hand touched her back as the mattress sunk beside her. "Sharon, my dear," Santa crooned, "what's wrong? No word from your sisters yet?"

She wanted to be left alone under her snowbank. Unwilling to move, she let out an affirmative groan but regretted it. Answering his question invited the problem-solving side of Santa, and he'd be there until he did.

The mattress shifted. "They probably haven't gone there yet. Something might have held them up. Maybe they don't know anything."

Ceding her isolation, Sharon rolled to her side. "But why don't they answer my texts?"

Santa's twinkling eyes widened a little and he shrugged. "Possibly they don't think you can handle what they found. They're trying to protect your feelings."

Heat flashed through her, forcing her to sit up. "Quit taking their side of it! I can handle it! I'm not made of tinsel!"

Santa shrunk back slightly, the twinkle in his eye faded slightly.

Her heart sank. She'd whacked her best friend with her angry inner turmoil. "I feel forgotten." It was the best apology she could muster without bursting into tears. To hold them back, she focused her attention on his red suspenders where they wrinkled the white shirt across his jelly-belly and his shoulders. His cotton work shirts added to her ironing chores on wash day. She'd tried to persuade him to wear tee shirts and lighten her ironing load. He said it was what he'd always worn. She'd try again.

Her hand went to her forehead to iron out the lines she knew were there, trying not to think about the argument coming with the conflicting need of her freedom from ironing a stack of shirts weekly and his freedom to wear whatever he chose to wear. Enough conflict crowded her calendar without adding more. She pushed away the thought so she could get back on track.

Desperate to do something—anything, she said, "I feel well enough to go back and check on them, but without the talisman, I'm stuck." Despondency forced her voice into a wail. "I should have stayed at Hannah's house until they knew about the cottage." Santa started to protest but she cut him off. "Don't you dare tell me I'd only have been in the way."

His woeful eyes sent regret through her. She'd whacked him again.

Santa stared at her, then stared at his hands. A heavy sigh hinted he'd grant her wish to be alone. He rose. "I might figure out a way to take you in the sleigh, but no promises.

The moon is near full, and it wouldn't be safe. I'm pretty sure NORAD won't approve my flight plan." Shoulders drooping, he went to the door.

Her strength returned, and she flung herself at him, throwing her arms around his wide neck. "I'm sorry, Santa dear! I know I'm asking a lot of you, but until this is resolved, I can't rest."

As he pried her arms away from him, his stern look startled her. "I said I'd try. I can't make any promises. Don't get mad at me if I don't succeed. Not everything is under my control." His jolliness was absent as he grumbled to himself. With an exasperated look, he left her alone.

With the door closed between them, she stuck her tongue out at him. "Can't make promises" were code words for he wasn't going to try very hard.

A rising emotional fever pushed her anxiety to the back burner, and she launched herself face down on the bed again. Her sisters were ignoring her, and she hated their silence. She'd done nothing wrong. Essie had procrastinated with calling their mother back for a last visit for so long, they'd lost the opportunity to do it. She was always too busy. It was too late, and her untimeliness forced a hardship on everyone else. How selfish could a person be!

And Hannah. She was no help. She'd been going to the cottage on the sly, taking the money and who knows what else to her house. She'd broken their promise to not visit the cottage unless she and Essie could go. Trusting her was out of the question.

Now her talisman was gone, stranding her in her home. So much for having sisters. A black cloud gathered over Sharon, rumbling in response to her thoughts.

The door squeaked slightly, followed by Santa's voice. "It's a no go on the sleigh. You're stuck here until they find your talisman, or the new moon comes around."

Sharon rolled over to stare at him, almost wishing she could give him a little zap for not bringing good news. Santa mumbled an apology and quickly closed the door. The dark cloud billowed and rose, fueled by anger and panic over being out of control. A thunderclap, and the emotional storm released its power in a downpour.

Chapter 13

Hannah

Old habits sometimes caused problems. Hannah wanted to cross her arms but being handcuffed to a chair prevented her from doing it. That frustration added another log to the fire burning inside her. She sat alone on a folding chair as people came and went out of the tent sheltering National Guard and sheriff department personnel. They'd caught several people looting as they patrolled the hurricane-damaged areas. They had no reason to think she wasn't one of them.

Her requests to see Officers Stanus and Hanover had gone ignored. Her cell phone was confiscated so reaching out for help wasn't an option. If anyone checked on her, she'd demand her one phone call. Headless would save her from this predicament. She'd also demand the return of the talisman. The last time she saw it, it lay beside a laptop, out in the open where anyone could take it. She'd tried to inch her way to it but was stopped by someone who noticed her new position in the room.

To make matters worse, they'd sent out extra patrols to search for the looter who got away. Essie. The radio crackled descriptions of her, followed by responses of negative reports on spotting her. They'd grilled her on where her companion went. She told them the truth: she was probably back in Germany in her underground house, trembling under her bed. They'd never find her in Florida. They were wasting their time. Their snorts of disgust and threats of jail time for not cooperating annoyed her as much as horse manure tracked across her clean kitchen floor.

No words could describe her feelings for Essie. The cowardly sister who abandoned her when their situation took a turn. Today marked the end of their friendship and sisterhood. From now on, she had no sister named Essie. She'd caused nothing but trouble. They'd lost their parents because of her. There remained no forgiveness for her actions and inactions.

With nothing else to do, she watched the hubbub as it swirled around her. Radios crackled as the various outposts checked in. Large parties of state and national disaster aid agencies wandered around, discussing their estimates of the damage. Nearby, a two-person call center fielded calls from landowners wondering what happened to their homes. A garbage can overflowed with empty cups, pop cans, food wrappers, and other debris left by the cyclone of workers.

Her back aching, Hannah played with the handcuffs holding her to the folding chair. She could pick the chair up and take off but wouldn't get far. The talisman around her neck called to her. She and the chair could snap home. If only she hadn't given her name to the National Guardsman who brought her here. He'd probably written her up in some sort of report so sooner or later, the law would come looking for her.

What she wanted to do most was to pick the handcuff lock, snap to wherever Essie had gone, and handcuff Essie to the chair. She deserved it. Her chest burned at the thought of being left behind by her spineless sister. The sister she thought had enough courage to stay. What a disappointment she turned out to be.

She stood and kicked the chair, an action she regretted after her arm was yanked and her toe hurt. The bustle in the canvas tent momentarily stopped as all eyes fell on her. Her cheeks felt hot. She folded up the chair, put it on the sand, and sat beside it. It was more comfortable than the chair.

The anger made her ears sensitive to the continual buzz around her—the ringing phones, people talking over each other, the vehicles coming and going. Noises filled her ears in spite of her trying to block them out. She'd almost succeeded until a sound rose above the rest. A voice she thought she'd never hear again. A screeching worse than fingernails on a blackboard and twice as grating.

Lifting herself up to peer over the table, there she was in her overstuffed finery. Elvira McKinzor. Sleezy realtor and empress pretender.

Quickly ducking again, Hannah's heart cringed. The last time she'd seen Elvira, she was in a dead faint over seeing Headless carrying his head while their ghost friends Rummy Jones and Peg Leg floated around her. Elvira's shyster lawyer friend, Howie Howard, and his crony, Ed, had to carry her out of the cottage and stuff her into his car. Her funny memory was likely Elvira's biggest nightmare and humiliation.

"I need to know how my properties fared during the storm." Elvira's voice demanded attention from the scurrying people. Most ignored her. A few got too close to her, and she grabbed them by an arm and made her demands. She didn't seem to care if she disturbed a volunteer or someone with some semblance of authority. She felt it was her right to hold them back from their assignments. Hannah couldn't hear the responses to her repeated demand, but Elvira's tone left little to be imagined.

The last thing Hannah wanted was to face Elvira in this environment, but her options were few. A better hiding place was needed. Hannah slowly pushed herself up and pulled the chair along the sandy floor of the tent, putting as much distance between her and the ranting Elvira as possible. Reaching the end of the table and the edge of the tent, she settled into the sand, hoping the tabletop was enough to hide her from Elvira's eyes.

The tent edge didn't quite reach the sand, leaving room for a breeze to make its way under. She lightly pushed on the tent hem, hoping it was loose enough to slide under. The canvas was far heavier than she thought and had little give, cutting off that option. Settling back, she waited and listened.

As she caught another hapless person by the arm, Elvira's voice rang through the tent above the hubbub. The person explained she needed to get supplies to someone, but Elvira would have none of it. "I don't care if you have time. Do you know who I am?" A pause. "Are you from out of state? You need to know who I am. I'm Elvira McKinzor, and you'll do well to remember that. I'm very important around here. I own a lot of property in this area, and I know our congresswoman, our governor, and our mayor, to name a few. None of them will be pleased to hear I wasn't kept abreast of the condition of my holdings."

The young woman wriggled her arm free and scurried off, leaving Elvira sputtering about her rudeness and inefficiencies.

From under the table, Hannah watched her fat legs and red sandals move around the tent, no doubt looking for someone else to listen to her complaints. Her heart began pounding when the red sandals moved her way. The chair held her in place with its unwieldiness. There was no escape from the eyes of Elvira.

"What do we have here?"

Hannah bit her lip, wanting to fade into the sand and out of sight, but escape was impossible. Slowly lifting her eyes, a bedazzled Elvira, hands on hips and a smirk on her face, came into view. Hannah conjured a speck of courage, picked up the chair, and stood as if sitting in the sand handcuffed to a chair were fashionable. "Hello, Elvira," she said as she held her voice steady. "Fancy meeting you here."

"Where are your weird friends?" A glint of fear flashed through Elvira's eyes as she looked around as if expecting to see something come through the side of the tent.

"They're busy at the moment."

Satisfied, Elvira stared at the chair in Hannah's hand. A snake-like grin covered her face as she saw the handcuffs. "How unexpected to see you, crawling in the sand like a crab. What brings you and your chair here?" Her eyes narrowed. "I didn't appreciate the stunt you pulled on Howie and me. You caused us a lot of trouble."

Hannah met her former foe's gaze with equal ferocity. "You should've believed us when we said we didn't want to sell Mother's cottage. We wanted no part of your scheme, but you kept coming back. You left us no choice. It was the only way to get rid of you." She got a better grip on the chair in case she needed to use it.

Elvira stepped forward enough to bump Hannah with her large chest. "I got friends with connections who could take care of you for good."

Repulsed, Hannah stepped back and held the chair between them. "You don't want to get into a fight with me, old lady. I have lots of friends too who would love to cast a spell on you and haunt you until the day you die."

A masculine voice interrupted their standoff. "What's going on here?" Firm hands on their shoulders pushed them apart.

Without breaking eye contact with Hannah, Elvira replied, "Nothing. Just talking with an old acquaintance."

Hannah wasn't letting her off that easy. "This woman tried to steal our cottage and property from us. Ask her if the place where you picked me up is mine. She knows it is. No wait—she's a liar and cheat. You can't trust anything she says."

An evil grin moved the corners of Elvira's mouth and her eyes narrowed. "Yes, I know where she lived, but of course, I have no idea where you picked her up. Knowing her, she was likely trying to loot one of my properties out of spite. She wasn't nice to me the last time we met."

A tsunami of anger roared through Hannah as she lifted the chair. "You—" the words fought against her lips to come out while her hands gripped the chair, ready to swing it. "You tried to steal our mother's cottage. You're mad because we stopped you and your lackey Howie from succeeding."

Elvira let out a soft, sarcastic chuckle. "I'm a respected realtor and developer. Ask the mayor. He knows me. As for this one…" she flitted a finger toward Hannah "…she owns the crazy woman's cottage that's haunted."

The National Guardsman's eyebrows went up as he looked at Hannah. "You own the crazy woman's cottage?"

Hannah swung the chair in her hand so it hit the table with a loud boom. Everyone stopped and stared at them. "You will not refer to my mother as a crazy woman!"

Elvira and the Guardsman took a step back.

The action gave Hannah impetus to continue. "She was a kind woman who liked her privacy. And yes, Sergeant, it's my house. You know I was on my property, release me. You have nothing to hold me on."

Elvira dug in her enormous bag and pulled out a business card. "Sergeant, here's where you can reach me when I can go see how my properties are doing. As for her..." she pointed at Hannah "...I'd hang on to her until you find out for sure she wasn't looting something of mine." With a triumphant look, she spun and left Hannah and the sergeant staring after her swaying backside.

Chapter 14

Essie

"What are you doing here?"

Essie spun around to face Easter in their bedroom. He came inside, shutting the door behind him. The noise of the children was muffled, but more importantly, her presence was hidden from them. Her body still shook with fear of going to jail for not having a passport. Guilt also had a stranglehold on her. She'd deserted Hannah, leaving her to face whatever punishment the law paid out. Her knees trembled, sending tremors through her. Tears and a sob erupted at the same time. She tumbled into Easter's arms.

Words tumbled out in a jumble. "Cottage gone…found clock…caught by the…police. They said…we shouldn't be there…digging in the cottage. They asked for…identification… I didn't have any…going to jail." It was all she had in her.

"What happened to Hannah? Did she snap home too?"

Essie shook her head.

"Where is she?"

"She's—she's still there. I had no identification."

Easter pushed her back. "You left her there?" His voice was high pitched, one he used when he was upset.

Already feeling guilty, Essie felt her brain go into self-defense mode. "Don't you get it? I didn't have a passport! I was an illegal alien. You know what the United States does with illegal aliens? Locks them up and forgets about them? I had to leave. I had no choice!"

Easter rubbed his face while his jaw muscles worked like the machinery in his factory in the height of Easter egg production. Essie stood watching him, waiting for the developing explosion. He didn't seem to care if she got thrown into jail or not. All he cared about was Hannah, the sister who took their mother's money. Whatever he had to say to her, she'd give him a piece of it back.

When he spoke, his voice was softer than she expected. "Get your passport and go back."

"What?" Her ears must not have been working properly. He wanted her to go back into the danger zone.

He squared himself in front of her. His tone was low and firm. "Get your passport and go back. You can't leave your sister hanging like a sheet in the wind. I can't believe you did." He waved his hand. "Go on. Go back to wherever you left her. She needs you. Once she's safe, come back. Or call me if you need help."

"Go back and be arrested?" Essie's voice came out like one of her children's pleas for mercy. "I'll be going to prison for a long time."

"They might deport you, but they won't put you in jail. Go back and help Hannah. You owe it to her."

Words failed Essie. If he'd blown up at her, she was ready to defend herself. But this soft voice and urgency to protect her sister wasn't what she wanted. She'd rather yell and scream at him for not understanding. The argumentative rug had been pulled out from under her.

"Do you know where your passport is?" he asked, eyebrows raised in desire for an answer.

She couldn't help but roll her eyes. "Of course, I do." She went to her music box and took out a key. It opened the lockbox hidden under the bed where she took her passport out with a flourish and waved it in front of Easter.

"Fine. Get going," he said as he stepped toward the bedroom door. "Find a way to call me before you come back. I'll have to explain something to the children, especially if you're sent to jail." He blew her a mocking kiss before he exited.

"Fine!" she yelled after him. Taking a pillow from the bed, she threw it at the door. The sound of children's voices in the hallway spurred her to action. She quickly locked up and put the key away. Her clothes were sandy and dirty. A shower and fresh change would feel good but wasn't the best thing to do. Hannah would be furious with her for leaving. Going back freshly groomed would only make her anger hotter.

With her passport in her pocket and the talisman in her hand, Essie stopped short of saying the chant as a new thought hit her. Hannah might have followed her lead and gone home right after she left. She was a clever woman and was probably safe at home. She and Headless were probably discussing the situation now. And because she was mad at her, Hannah hadn't called to tell her so.

Convincing herself that Hannah at home, Essie decided that instead of going to Florida, she'd go to Hannah's house and set things straight. A sincere apology might set things right. Her body relaxed as she realized everything was going to turn out fine. She'd be home in time to tell her children good night. She said the chant and added, "Hannah's house."

With a spin and a squeeze, she found herself standing in Hannah's living room. The house was still, with only the humming of the refrigerator and muted birds' songs to break the silence. "Hannah?" she said softly hoping for an answer. Getting none, she went to the kitchen window and looked out toward the barn. She saw Headless grooming a black horse in the corral.

"Whatcha looking for, dearie?" a voice creaked behind her.

Like a tornado, Essie spun around to see a gray-haired woman crouched over, looking up at her in a sideways manner. Essie grabbed her chest so her wildly beating heart wouldn't jump out and run off to the barn. The woman's nose curved down as her chin rose to meet it. Her scalp reflected the light from the window through the thin, scraggly hair. She looked like the short female counterpart of Quasimodo.

One of the woman's eyes looked Essie up and down. "Ah, ya must be one of dear Hannah's sisters. I see a resemblance."

Essie swallowed hard and whispered, "I am. And who are you?"

The stump of a woman cackled like a crow. "I'm the Horseman's neighbor. They call me Mrs. Hagg. What's your name?"

Relief at hearing a familiar name helped calm Essie's flight impulse. "I'm Essie Bunny, Hannah's older sister. Nice to meet you. I've heard a lot about you. Is Hannah here?"

She shook her head as she made her way to the laundry room door.

Essie heard a shrill whistle that could have shattered nearby eardrums. Through the kitchen window, she saw Headless trotting toward the house, the hellhounds hot on his heels. She took the talisman in hand.

"Don't use that just yet, dearie." Mrs. Hagg's crooked grin wrinkled her face more than it already was. "Headless will want to know you're here."

Headless wouldn't be pleased with her. She could already feel the heat of his wrath for her abandoning Hannah in their time of need. The temptation to say the chant and flee from the impending wrath was strong, but Mrs. Hagg's insistence she stay was stronger. Easter was right; she should have gone to Florida. If she'd asked the talisman to take her to Hannah, things would have worked out better.

The back door opened, and the hounds came bouncing in, running to Mrs. Hagg who greeted them as friends. They were nearly as tall as the little woman.

As soon as Headless walked in, Mrs. Hagg started telling him what had happened to Hannah, spilling the news out like she'd been there.

Essie stood anchored to the spot. How could this little woman know what had happened?

Headless looked at Mrs. Hagg, then looked at Essie, his mouth open. He waved his hand to get her to slow her speaking. "Wait, Hannah's where? I thought she was with you, Essie?" When Mrs. Hagg repeated what she'd said, he cried out, "Great flaming pumpkins! I've got to get to her!"

A hot flash of embarrassment and shame crawled up Essie's neck and into her face. "I'm sorry! They asked for our IDs and I had nothing. I was an illegal alien and you know what they do with those. I was afraid of being thrown into jail somewhere and forgotten. I went home to get my passport." Pulling it out of her pocket, she waved it around for them to see. "I'll go back and face whatever is coming for us."

Before she finished her spiel, Headless had his phone out trying to call Hannah. "No answer." He pulled his own talisman out of his shirt pocket and said, "I'll be back when I find her." Turning, he looked at Mrs. Hagg. "Is she safe?"

The crooked woman's eyes glazed over. "She's fine, only aggravated at her sister." Her eyes cleared and stared at Essie.

Too ashamed to look at either of them, Essie hung her head. "The police probably have her phone. I'm sorry. I shouldn't have snapped away." Her nose started running the same time as tears dropped from her eyes.

Mrs. Hagg reached out her gnarled hand and held on to Essie's arm. "Your remorse is real." Turning to Headless, she stated, "Hannah still has her talisman. She's delayed but not in trouble yet. If things get worse, she'll be able to come back here." She turned to Essie. "You should go back."

Essie felt her forehead wrinkle up as she scratched her head. How did this little woman know what was going on with Hannah? Before she could ask, Headless answered her question.

"Mrs. Hagg is clairvoyant," he whispered as he moved beside her. "She has remarkable gifts, and she shares them with us."

The little woman smiled, revealing her snaggled brown teeth. Essie smiled back at her, not wanting to incur her disagreement. She hoped her smile seemed real. Hannah often said Mrs. Hagg had a heart of gold. Anyone who shared their extrasensory gifts was probably one of the good guys, but it was hard not to stare at the strange-looking little woman.

Tearing her eyes away, Essie told them, "I came here, hoping she had left right after me. Since I know Hannah's not here, I'm going back to Florida."

"The story has a familiar ring," Headless murmured as he took his talisman in hand again. "Let me go. She'll clobber you when she sees you.

A crooked finger pointed at Headless. "It's not your mission. Let her sister go back and finish what she must." Turning to Essie, the strange little woman asked, "You lost one of the talismans, didn't you."

A streak of fear stirred Essie's heart to beat even faster. "Sharon lost it when the clock fell on her. Hannah and I found it, but it was taken away by one of the policemen who took us back to their headquarters."

"You found it?" Headless took a step closer. One of the dogs nuzzled his hand, and he scratched his ears.

"Yes! We found it under the clock. We'd dug out the workings and the face and were trying to free the pendulum when we were interrupted by two guards. They said we were looting and took us to a central dispatch place. One of them took the talisman and put it in his pocket. I'm not sure what he did with it after that."

Mrs. Hagg let out a sound and squeezed her hands together. "It's of no use to the man. It only works for the person who first used it. It will work for no one else." She turned her attention to the dogs who eagerly accepted it.

Essie looked at her watch. It had been an hour since she left, plenty of time for Hannah to stew about being abandoned. Sooner or later, she had to face Hannah's fury. She'd done a cowardly thing, and an apology was in order when she was able to get in a word in during the expected tirade. Armed with her passport, she was ready to face the officers, but she wasn't ready to face her sister's wrath.

Without waiting to ask permission to leave, Essie held on to her talisman. "Pop my bubble—"

"Stop!" Headless pulled on her hand holding the talisman. "Let's think this thing through. What will you do when you get to Hannah?"

"Tell her I'm sorry for leaving and accept my punishment."

"Let me help," he said as he rushed into the living room. "Let's make a copy of something to show the cottage is yours and you're not looting."

"Better idea," Essie said as she rushed behind him.

He went to an office and dug through a file cabinet. He pulled out an insurance statement with the address of the cottage. After a little more digging, he cried out in triumph and pulled out a property tax bill.

"This should prove to them you weren't looting anyone's property but your own." He stopped. "Maybe you should word that differently." He made copies of the documents and handed them to Essie. "Take these with you. They should help."

Folding them and putting them in her pocket, Essie felt better. "Thanks for that. They have nothing on us, and we can prove it. Plus, Hannah may not kill me, only maim." She lifted her talisman but stopped. "You've been kinder to me than Easter was. He was furious I left Hannah there alone."

Headless pursed his lips together, tapped his foot, and relayed, "Let's say I'm not happy about it, but I understand it. Now please, get going. And tell her I'm anxious to have her home." His eyes were getting red, and his mouth was starting to get the jagged lines of a pumpkin.

Seeing his anger control melting, Essie was not eager to press the issue. Armed with proof of ownership and her passport, Hannah's rescue was in her hands. She said the chant and snapped away.

Chapter 15

Sharon

Sharon's room was dark, reflecting her mood. No one bothered her when the lunch hour came and passed. Her stomach grumbled its protest, and she pulled the belt on her robe tighter. Perturbed but thankful at the same time, she was glad for the solitude.

She crawled off the bed and stood at her window looking out across the frozen tundra. The day-old snowfall sparkled and glistened in the sunlight. The sparkle would last for only a few more weeks before the sun left for the southern skies. The stars would take over the job, sparkling and twinkling their beauty in the dark skies. Christmas would come close behind.

The scene filled Sharon's eyes with good things, but inside, she was still feeling cast aside by her sisters. Neither of them returned her calls or texts. Her anger at being stuck at home pushed aside her panic of uncertainty. Her emotions were on a teeter-totter, one up and the other down, the other would rise while the other fell. Equilibrium seemed impossible.

Where were Hannah and Essie? Had they found the clock? When would they bring it here to see if the elves could repair it? The strength of her panic began to rise, pushing anger aside and leaving her clutching her chest and gasping. A paper bag sat on the chair. Grabbing it, she worked to calm her nerves. Whatever concoction Corina had for helping with this, she was determined to try.

The door opened behind her, making her anger help squash the panic. Nothing in the world could make her want to see anybody right now. She would defend her solitude to the last—

"Sharon, Headless is here," Santa's voice boomed out. "He's come for you."

Hope gushed up like a geyser. Throwing the bag aside, she adjusted her robe to be more presentable. Her tall brother-in-law come in the door behind Santa who flipped on the light. Blinking in the brightness and knowing she must look awful, she finger-combed her hair while she shielded her eyes. "Headless, welcome. What brings you here?"

"How are you feeling, Sharon?" He walked over with his hand extended as he pushed back the hood on his jacket. As he shook her hand, he asked, "Feel like coming to my house?"

Santa stepped to her side. "But only if you're feeling okay. I don't want you to go if you haven't recovered from the other day. And take a true assessment of how you feel." He looked at Headless. "She doesn't have an off button, and she'll run herself into the ground if we don't watch her."
Stepping back and crossing his arms, Headless replied, "I'll keep a close eye on her and make her rest."

Picking a piece of lint off his flannel shirt, Santa said, "I'd go, but the workshop is in full production."

The men stood, looking at Sharon holding her robe close around her. "You've got nothing to worry about. Mrs. Hagg and I will take good care of her."

The attention annoyed her. They talked like she wasn't standing there. True, she wasn't quite up to normal feeling, but she didn't want to be stuck here anymore. If Headless took her back to his house, she'd gladly go. "I feel fine. Get out of here and let me get changed." She swooshed them away.

In record time, she surveyed herself in the mirror. Her black slacks and light blue tunic would bring a smile to her sisters' faces. Their first visit together had given her a broader taste in clothing styles and colors. Lipstick and a few extra paper bags in her purse and she was ready to go.

Santa and Headless were talking in low tones in the hallway. They looked up as she came out of the bedroom. They motioned her back inside and followed.

"We're keeping it a secret that you're leaving," Santa said before he gave her a peck on the cheek. "Headless will bring you back if you start feeling bad or weak or sick." He bent over to look her square in the face. "You tell him the truth on how you feel. No hero stuff."

With assurances from the tall man, Santa seemed to relax a little. Santa gave Sharon a good-bye kiss on the lips while Headless secured the hoodie tightly around his face. He held his talisman out and said, "Ready?"

Excitement pushed the first smile on her face for days. Taking a hold of the talisman, she replied, "Let's do it."

Headless put his arm around her and held her tight as he said the chant. The squeezing stopped when she felt a floor under her feet, but the spinning in her head continued a little longer. Strong arms helped her stumble to a chair until the vertigo passed.

"Do you need one of your bags?"

Sharon waved off his question, determined to conquer this momentary problem. As the spinning subsided, she laughed. "That ride gets more exciting each time I take it." She watched Headless remove his jacket and reset his head on its cradle. "While I wait for my balance to return, why don't you fill me in on what's going on?"

146

As Headless gave her the latest news, he prepared a snack of veggies, sandwiches, and chips. Essie and Hannah had found the clock and unburied it. Essie had returned to Hannah's location, but he didn't know what had happened after her return. He too was waiting for news from them. He'd given Essie strict orders for them to return home if the situation warranted. "We're hoping with the papers, they'll be able to persuade them to release them. It's proof they weren't looting."

Sharon's stomach cried out in a loud roar for food as it was set in front of her. Warmth spread over her cheeks as she sneaked a chip to quiet it. When Headless motioned for her to dig in, she quickly accepted the invitation, filling her plate with a taste of it all. Her hand stopped on its way to her mouth when Mrs. Hagg walked into the room and sat across from her. The unexpected sight startled Sharon, turning her to stone as if looking at Medusa's face.

"Sharon, this is our neighbor, Mrs. Hagg. Mrs. Hagg, this is Hannah's other sister, Sharon Claus," he said as he poured iced tea for them.

A shrieky voice came across the table. "Ah, yes, I see the resemblance. You're the one who's scared all the time." Piling her plate with food, she dove in with the gusto of a woman set free from a strict diet.

Freed from her petrification, Sharon choked out, "Nice to meet you." Averting her eyes, she took a bite of sandwich so she wouldn't have to engage in conversation. The pleas of Horace and Huntley not to be left alone with Mrs. Hagg made sense now. From Hannah's unwavering support of her, this troll-like woman was a friend of hers. Heart of gold, she thought she'd heard Hannah say. She mustn't be naughty and offend a friend. Her brain kept repeating a friend of Hannah's, a friend of Hannah's...

Smacking her lips, Mrs. Hagg swallowed and said, "You lost your talisman."

Sharon stopped chewing, startled by the abrupt declaration but continued when she figured Headless had already told her about it. Nodding seemed the proper required response.

"Can't make you another one." Tiny food bits fell from her mouth as she spoke. "Only one per person." She gave Sharon a sideways glance.

Sharon quickly looked away, more from the disgusting eating habits than from her appearance. Her heart sank. The end of her snapping wherever she wanted was over. She'd made many shopping forays with the talisman, especially before Christmas. She and Santa had gone to see their son Sam at college several times with it. The travel device was used often and treasured. It was much easier than asking NORAD for permission to take the sleigh. Its absence was a devasting loss.

Sharon stared at her now tasteless food.

"But I can help you find it."

The crackled voice was closer than she knew. Sharon looked out of the side of her eyes into the green cat-like gaze of Mrs. Hagg. A crooked closed-lip smile was on her face. Inside Sharon, a glimmer of hope shone like the first star at night. "I'd like your help."

Mrs. Hagg sat back in her chair and cackled like a hen, with a mouthful of food exposed for any lookers to see. How Hannah saw a heart of gold in this crude woman was almost beyond Sharon's comprehension, but still, willingness to help a stranger meant she wasn't all bad.

Chapter 16

Hannah

Hannah sipped the bottled water someone had been nice enough to bring her. Her backside ached from sitting in the hard folding chair. She'd heard her cell phone ringing numerous times but was denied the chance to answer. Headless was calling, she was sure, looking for her and wondering why she wasn't back yet. Several times, she'd tried to muster some unknown force in her attempt to levitate the phone to her. She'd seen it work in a movie, but so far, no success.

People came and went. The sides of the tent were rolled up to let air move freely. The activity around her declined as more news was released to the public. The phones rang less. Calls were rerouted to another location. People waved goodbye as they left to go somewhere else. Still, Hannah sat there, waiting, waiting for something to happen with her.

A lull in the ringing phones opened an opportunity for her. "Hey you!" she shouted at a younger man with a headset on. He looked at her and pointed his finger toward his chest. "Yes, you! Come here!"

Unplugging his headset, he came over and stood across the table from her. She grabbed him by his souvenir tee shirt and pulled his face close to hers. "I've been here for hours," she growled through clenched teeth. "Either give me my phone or let me go."

The man's eyes widened. "But I—but I—" He tried to pull back, but Hannah's vise grip wouldn't let him go.

"Use your headset..." she flipped the coiled cord up, making it hit him in the nose "...and call either Officer Stanus or Officer Hanover to come here and release me. Do it NOW!" She released her grip on his shirt.

A man with a badge came up behind the young man and pulled him away. He patted the young man on the back and told him to take a break. "Ma'am, we're still looking for your companion who got away. If you'd like to tell us where she is, things would go faster." He leaned across the table toward her. His name tag shone in the light. Cooper it read. Three stripes decorated his sleeve. "Cooperation goes a long way toward release."

Hannah leaned toward him. "And again, I say to you, I have no idea where she is. She deserted me."

"You need to pick better friends." He leaned back and laughed. His laughter continued to ring out as he left the area.

Her nerves already frayed, she had to grit her teeth to keep a scream from jumping out and filling the tent. She could pick her friends, but she was stuck with her no-good sister. When she saw Essie again, she'd—wait, she didn't want to see Essie ever again. After this betrayal, there would be no relationship with this sister. No more waiting on her or listening to her constant excuses for her foot dragging. She almost felt lighter.

A familiar snap sounded behind her. There was the sister she never wanted to see again, excitedly whispering in her ear.

"I'm back. Sorry it took so long. Headless sent papers with me to prove we own the land."

Biting her bottom lip, Hannah turned to glare at the excited face of Essie. Laser eyes seemed the appropriate response to the unwelcome guest.

Essie's happy expression faded but shone again as she dug in her pocket and pulled out folded papers. With a flick of her wrist, she fanned them in front of Hannah. "We have proof we own the cottage. Headless copied the tax and insurance forms for me to bring. He said—"

"You saw Headless? Is that where you've been while I've been sitting here…" she held up her wrist "…chained to a chair?"

Essie backed away as her face fell. She plopped into the sand beside Hannah's chair. "I admit it. I panicked. I didn't have any identification papers with me, and I was afraid of going to jail. I'm very sorry." On cue, she sniffed and wiped an eye.

Having one fearful sister was enough. Hannah wasn't letting Essie off the hook that easily. The handcuff prevented her from crossing her arms. Instead, she turned her back on Essie and crossed her legs.

"But I'm here now," Essie pleaded. "I know I did wrong. People around the world are mad at me. Easter had a fit I left. After getting my passport, I went to your house hoping you'd be there, but when you weren't and I was, Headless isn't too happy with me either. He thought the papers—"

"Aha!"

Hannah's body jerked at the loud noise. When she turned to look, all she saw was a silver star shining in the light reflected off the ocean. Without looking up, she knew it was Cooper back to check on her and to ask again about Essie's whereabouts.

As he leaned over the table to look at Essie on the sand, he said, "The escaped looter has returned."

Essie looked from Cooper to Hannah and back. "I didn't escape. I went home—er, I went to her house…" she pointed at Hannah "…and got the papers showing we were on property we own." She waved them at him.

Eyeing the papers, he asked, "How did you get in and out of here without being seen?"

In a sandy fit, Essie stood up. "I used magic." She waved her hand wildly. "Never mind that. We're not looters, and I have proof of it." She spun the unfolded papers across the table toward the officer. "We own the property where you rudely interrupted us while we were saving our mother's clock. I demand you release my sister and let us go our own way." She gave Hannah a triumphant look.

"I can verify it too," came a voice from behind the officer. Stepping around him, Officer Jessica Hanover faced the two sisters, feet apart and hands resting on her utility belt. "Still driving ghosts around in your van? Or are you harassing realtors who want to buy your haunted cottage?" Cooper stood up and waved his finger at the sisters. "You know these two?"

"Oh yeah." Officer Hanover crossed her arms and rocked on her heels. "We've had several run-ins with them. Always a little weird. A little eerie. A lot of creepy."

"Nice to see you again," Hannah said trying to smile in a friendly manner. Although she was miffed at having to wait so long for Officer Hanover to show up, there was no sense in torqueing her off now. At least there were no disembodied voices coming out of the air or pirate ghosts around to flick her mic chord like they'd done before.

"This one…" Cooper pointed at Essie "…said she used magic to get in and out of here." He pointed at his ear and made circles with his finger, the universal sign of crazy.

Giving a slight nod, Officer Hanover's eyes flitted around as if expecting a disembodied voice to give an opinion. Her hand went to the cord on her shoulder radio. "If you're smart, you'll let them go. They're trouble." She turned to go but stopped and said over her shoulder, "Trouble but not in an unlawful way. A supernatural way." Then she was gone.

Cooper eyed the two like they were hardened criminals getting away with murder. Pulling a key from his pocket, he unlocked the handcuffs holding Hannah to the chair. "Get out of here and stay away until this area is open to the homeowners. We've got enough to do without having to deal with people who are weird, but not unlawful." He waved them away and they granted his wish as fast as their feet could carry them.

The sunlight was hot on her back as Hannah hurried through the tents, pallets of supplies, and vehicles around the disaster headquarters. She stopped when she saw Officer Hanover talking to someone ahead. The police officer stepped to the side and Elvira came into view. Essie ran into the back of her, almost sending both of them to the ground. Hannah pushed her sister behind a pile of crates.

Shushing her inquisitive sister, Hannah crawled to the edge of their hiding place. Elvira was unhappy the sisters had been released. Trying to go around the whining woman, Officer Hanover kept repeating there were no charges to hold them on. When she finally got around the large glitter-covered woman, Hanover took off like she was chasing a fleeing felon.

Hannah sat back against the crate. Without saying a word to Essie, she pulled out her talisman and recited the chant to go home. A squeezing, a spinning, and the floor of her living room came under her feet. She'd barely got her bearings and started to stand when someone behind her knocked her off balance.

"Oops," Essie said, "Sorry about that. I didn't know I'd land in the same spot as you."

Heat surged through her like electricity as she turned to face her sister. "Why are you here? Go to your own home!" Turning her back, she was done talking to her older sister who'd abandoned her in a time when they needed to stand strong together. She might have brought the papers, but Officer Hanover got better results than they did. No, she was done with Essie forever.

Headless came trotting out of the kitchen, followed closely by Mrs. Hagg. "You're back!"

Encircled by the arms of her husband, Hannah felt the stress of her ordeal melt away like ice on a scorching day. Everyone disappeared, leaving the two of them to love and—

"Did the papers Essie brought do the trick?"

Headless broke the magical place she was in. She pushed back from him, ready to smack the next one who annoyed her. The mercury in her temper thermometer rose higher and higher as Essie became the center of attention telling her version of the events leading to Hannah's release. Knowing how and why Sharon and Mrs. Hagg were there was less important than seeing how deftly Essie moved herself from villain to rescuer. The shoulder hug Headless gave her was the last straw.

"That's it!" Hannah took a step, spread her feet into a superhero stance, and rubbed her fist. "It sounds very moving, but no one is mentioning I—yes, I—was left alone there to face Officer Cooper by myself. Essie might have brought the papers, but I'M—" she beat her chest with her finger "—I'm the one who was handcuffed to a chair, not knowing if or when anyone would help me. She's not the brave one. I am!"

She stood a moment, expecting accolades for her bravery. She got nothing but stares and silence until Headless put his arm around her shoulder.

"You're definitely the brave one." He released her and said, "Did you bring Sharon's talisman with you?"

Closing her eyes, Hannah barked, "No."

Sharon's eyes well up as she let out a cry of disappointment. The others immediately rushed to her.

Stunned, Hannah walked into the kitchen, through the laundry room, and out the back door. They wouldn't miss her with precious Essie and whiny Sharon around.

She rubbed the red ring around her wrist where the handcuffs had been. Her private conversation with herself took the whole distance to the barn. First Essie deserted her and now Headless. He seemed enthralled with the supposed bravery of Essie returning to rescue her. She didn't need rescuing. Once Officer Hanover showed up, she'd have been released so in reality, Essie bringing those stupid papers did little good.

A horse nickered as Hannah approached the corral. Climbing over the fence, Hannah joined her favorite mare. The horse nuzzled her arm and responded with a gentle nudge when Hannah scratched her neck. Seeing a comb nearby, she got it and pulled it through the long mane and tail of the black mare. An occasional scratch and pat made the mare's eyes close partway as it stood still for grooming. Her corral-mates came over to nuzzle Hannah for their own grooming desires. Rubs and pats seemed to make them happy.

"It's safe for you to come back to the house."

Hannah looked over the back of the mares to see Headless, his forearms supporting him as he leaned on the top rail of the corral. A mare lowered her head in front of her, requesting an ear scratching. She fulfilled the request only to be pestered by the others wanting the same treatment. Giving each one a little comfort, she gave them one last pat before going to the fence. "I couldn't take it anymore. I had to leave."

He nodded and reached out to scratch a soft, black muzzle that had followed Hannah to the fence. "I know. Essie was proud of rescuing you—her word, not mine. I get why it bothers you. It started with Sharon's consuming worry over the clock and her staying behind. Then you get deserted by Essie when you need her most. I don't blame you for being angry with them."

His dark eyes hypnotized her. No longer able to blink, she knew he could look into her mind and see her thoughts. He was her calm voice when things got crazy.

A velvety nose nudged her hand, asking for a favor. The horse nudged harder, getting Hannah to look at it. The mare's head went up and down as if agreeing with Headless and urging her to do the same. A light laugh came out of her as she threw her arms around the black neck.

Headless joined the laughter. "Horses know best. Essie went home, and Mrs. Hagg took Sharon home. The boys will be home from school soon. Normal has returned to the Horseman household, that is if you're okay."

Climbing over the fence, Hannah walked toward the house with Headless by her side. "I'm okay, just traumatized by my sister who left me there. While she was gone, I decided I didn't want to see her anymore. I'm done with my sisters. Life was simpler without them around."

"You can't mean what you're saying. You were happy to reconnect with them. That feeling couldn't have changed in a single moment."

She stopped under an oak tree in their back yard. A tire swing hung there, reminding her of the days when her boys were younger. She missed those days when it was the four of them. Dividing her time and worries on her immediate family seemed less complicated. Sister relationships were too complex.

Holding Headless back before he went on, she told him, "We found the clock, but it's destroyed. The cottage is gone. There's nothing left to bind me and my sisters together. It's time to go our separate ways."

Chapter 17

Essie

The dinner table was silent. Essie sat at the other end mixing and remixing the salad on her plate. Without moving her head, she peeked at her family around the table. Forks sat were they'd been set, and food cooled on plates. Easter sat on the other end of the table, eyes down at his food. Lack of interest in supper was rarely a problem. Tension swirled above them like bees over a flower garden.

The squabble Essie and Easter had when she returned from Hannah's house hadn't been a pleasant one. He was more than unhappy with her instantaneous comings and goings, never knowing when she'd want to snap away, or when she'd be back. Running the factory and running the household when she was gone put him over the edge. He also had the added burden of coming up with excuses for the children on why she wasn't at home.

At the peak of the argument, he'd demanded to retain control of her talisman. Appalled by the request, she'd refused and told him he was a selfish, long-eared carrot sucker. From the look in his eyes, she'd gone way over the line with her words. He rushed out before she could apologize.

The table jerked slightly in rhythm with a child's sniffing. Thirteen children eyed each other, mouthed words across the table, and made subtle hand signals toward their parents at each end of the table. Only Alan and Jason showed any interest in the pork wiener schnitzel and potatoes on the table. Sitting next to each other, the tween-aged boys ate with gusto without any regard for the family drama upsetting everyone else.

The quiet was shattered when Easter slammed his fork on the table and said to his daughter sitting beside him, "Oh for all that's boiled and scrambled, Jenny, quit kicking the table, and get a tissue for your nose!"

With raised eyebrows, Essie gave him a don't-yell-at-my-daughter glare, but he didn't look her way. Dabbing the corners of her mouth with her napkin, she asked, "Jenny, you may go get a tissue."

The 9-year-old let out a howl like a bawling cow. "I don't need a tissue." She broke into sobs.

Easter threw his hands in the air. "What—why are—" His eyes met Essie's.

As confused as he was, she responded, "I have no idea."

Sylvie turned to her mother and said, "Mother, how can you be so insensitive!" She pushed her chair back and ran to Jenny and enveloped her in a hug.

The room suddenly grew hot, and she wiped a small bead of sweat from her upper lip. "Insensitive about what?" Sue, Stacy, and Sarah started sniffling and clung to each other. Clara sat unmoving, hard-faced, staring at the wall. Marcia and Pete, the oldest, were carrying on a private conversation while Jason and Alan continued to shovel more food on their plates.

"Hold it!" Easter stood and leaned on his fists on either side of his plate. "Family meeting! Stacy, get a box of tissues and pass it around. Everyone else, sit quietly and stop this nonsense." His fierce look went around the table and stopped on Essie.

Her heart skipped a beat but not a loving one. She knew when his limit had been reached and this time, it may have been stretched over the line a little too far. Pushing her plate away, she crossed her arms and waited to see how he handled this.

The tissue box was passed like a bowl of peas. Essie handed it off to Thomas on her right who passed it to Sadie on his right. When the box got back to Easter, he set it in his chair.

"Everyone have their tissues? Good. It's obvious something is going on behind your mother's and my back. Who wants to explain it?"

All eyes went to the alpha child, Pete. Throwing his napkin on top of his untouched meal, he pushed his chair back a little. "We want to know if you're getting a divorce."

Essie couldn't control it. Her eyes rolled on their own. "Kids, this is crazy—"

"Hush!" Easter glared at her, and she was sure she returned the same look. "You know the rules. At family meetings, everyone is allowed to speak without interruption."

Her face burned with being publicly chastised. Unwilling to let it be, her eyebrows went up, and she made a zipping motion across her lips.

Nodding to Pete, she faked a grin. Pete's worried look wiped her grin away. The argument was between her and Easter. Her innocent children were caught in the acid rain corroding their normally happy home. The back of her throat tensed up, bringing with it a downward look to hide her eyes as she blinked them rapidly.

"You and Mother are fighting all the time," Pete said softly but with the voice of a concerned adult. "Mother is gone a lot lately, and when she's here, you two argue. We can't help but hear it. It comes through your door."

Unable to look at her son as he stated his observations, she could feel his eyes on her. They deserved an explanation, but to give them one, she'd have to reveal the talisman to them. The agreement between Mrs. Hagg and the sisters was their husbands were the only ones who knew about the talismans. To break that trust might mean breaking the spell allowing her to travel with it. As mad as she was at her sisters, she treasured being able to go anywhere she wanted without paying for a seat on an airline. Instantaneous travel was too valuable to risk by sharing a secret.

Essie looked at Pete who was still talking. She'd lost track of what he'd said which sent a streak of dismay through her. Her response to the accusations relied on her listening. She squeezed her fingernails into her palms in punishment for letting her mind wander.

"We'd like to know if you and Mother are splitting up. I think we have a right to know." His jaw firmed as he looked at his parents. His siblings cheered his speech, some banging their silverware on the table to show their approval.

Easter held his hand up for silence. The regret in his eyes as he looked at Essie made her feel it too. Their disagreements had gone beyond the door of their bedroom and out into the house. They'd have to learn to either be quieter when they fought or find a compromise. Which would be easier was hard to tell.

"Anyone else care to say something before I turn the floor over to your mother?"

The children exchanged glances with each other. A few elbow nudges were traded but no one else volunteered to speak. Jenny and Sue wiped their eyes, and Sarah let out a jagged breath. The older girls, Marcia, Sylvie, and Clara stared at their hands, unmoving and seemingly emotionless until a tear dropped into Clara's lap. Sadie and Stacy leaned on each other, holding hands. Ned looked lost. Thomas and

Pete didn't know where to look. Jason and Alan chewed their food, looking at what was left to eat.

An invisible knife of guilt struck Essie's heart. Her focus on her own problems blinded her to the impact it was having on her children. It was Hannah's fault. If she'd taken care of the cottage like she was supposed to, this wouldn't be happening. Anger pushed guilt out of the way before steaming ahead.

Easter motioned for her to take the floor. Standing, she saw a spark of fear in her family's eyes. It was the same look she got when she was on the warpath about someone making a mess and not cleaning it up. The same look when she was hunting for someone who hadn't done their chores. The same look said they feared what would come next.

Her father's necklace hanging around her neck seemed to call to her. She took it in her hands and rubbed the pendant. It might bring her luck or better yet, the right words.

Clearing her throat, she began. "Your father and I disagree about certain things. It's part of being married. We're individuals who don't think the same way all the time." She looked for reactions, but her audience were statues, motionless and blank. "Just because we disagree doesn't mean we don't love each other. It means we have different opinions about an issue. That's it. No, we're not getting a divorce. No, we won't tell you what the argument is about. You'll have to trust me when I say it doesn't involve you."

She looked down at her salad that seemed so far away. Repositioning the silverware, she continued. "I'm sorry we bothered you. We'll try to do better." She sat, crossed her arms, and stared at the cold food on the table. Her extra efforts to make a nice meal had been ruined by the kids and the family meeting.

162

The silent uneasiness sent a shiver through Essie. Someone should say something. A clearing of his throat signaled Easter was ready to take control of the meeting again. "Thomas, remember the other day when you and Jason argued about whose turn it was to rake the yard? You yelled at each other about who was right. Did your argument mean you hated each other? No. It meant you each thought you were right and felt strongly about it. That's how it is with your mother and me. We disagree and feel strongly each of us is right. But divorce? It's never entered the conversation. I love your mother…"

His long pause made Essie look up to see what was going on. Tenderness and apology shone out of his eyes, eliciting a smile from her.

"…and I think she still loves me."

Essie nodded.

"Stop talking about this crazy idea about us splitting up because it's not happening. We're the Bunny family, and we stick together!"

A split second of hush was followed by the letting go of a collective breath, cries of relief, chattering about I-told-you-so, and shouts demanding to know what was for dessert. Laughter once again filled the dining room as the hungry children chowed down on tepid food but didn't seem to mind. Across the table, Easter gave Essie a wink.

Essie's nylon nightgown sparkled with static electricity as she got ready for bed in the dim light of her bedroom. Easter was already in bed with a book propped up in front of him, but his eyes weren't moving. His mind was clearly elsewhere.

"A euro for your thoughts," she said as she slipped under the covers beside him.

163

Closing the book, Easter reached beside him and turned out the light. His arm reached out to pull her in close. "I'm sorry about our fighting, but it's frustrating!" He rubbed his forehead. "I never know if you're here or somewhere on the other side of the globe. Whether you're safe or in trouble. I feel helpless!" He lay quiet for a minute. "I feel left out," he whispered.

Instead of being a loving hug, his arm felt like a lead weight around her. She used the talisman when circumstances dictated, not when she felt a whim. The feeling of being tied down overwhelmed her and she pushed his arm away. "I do what I have to do. Sometimes I can't wait for you to approve my every move. The storm was coming. You told me to go help. I did, but you got mad because it required more time than you thought. What am I supposed to do? Quit being a part of my sisters' lives? Stop caring about seeing my mother one last time?"

She knew the last barb would strike a nerve in him. His sigh that followed it let her know it had hit the mark, and she used the advantage. "Give me the freedom to go until we get the clock back together and the cottage rebuilt. After that, I'll stay home all the time." The last promise would be hardest to keep, but she'd renegotiate that point later. She'd take the chance.

He let out a soft laugh. "And you think I believe that? I know you. The next time one of your sisters calls, off you'll go."

"No, I'm done with my sisters. It's been nothing but trouble since we got back together. There's nothing between us now. No cottage. No clock. No calling—" the words caught in her throat. "—no calling Mother back one last time." Gripping her lower face, she refused to let the tears out.

164

A sigh escaped from Easter as he reached out his arm and drew her close again. "Don't you think that's rather drastic? You were so happy to have your sisters again. Why give up?"

"Because they don't like me. I've made a lot of mistakes."

"All forgivable in time."

She wasn't sure about that, but this wasn't the time to argue about it. Other topics needed attention more. "Will you give me my talisman back? I'll take care of it and not snap off anywhere without permission." She snuggled closer to him. "Once the kids are back in school, you and I can get away on mini-vacations any time we want. We wouldn't have to worry about paying for a hotel because we'll be back before they get home."

"Sounds exciting! Where should we go?"

Letting out a laugh, Essie snuggled against him again. "How about a trip to the United States to check on a clock?"

Chapter 18

Sharon

The master bedroom was as dark as Sharon's insides felt. She lay curled up on their big bed, unmoving, neither sleeping nor awake. Breathing and the ache in her chest were her only movement and feeling. The end had come, and she wasn't prepared to deal with it. Her sisters didn't like each other, and she didn't like them much. It was like the past few years hadn't happened and they were estranged again. Adding to her sorrow was the recurring dream of her father telling them to come together. Come together? They couldn't stand each other.

Her only pinprick of hope was if Mrs. Hagg could help her find her talisman. The strange little woman had powers Sharon didn't understand but was willing to use. She'd pretty much do anything to find her talisman again. Her sisters found it once when it seemed impossible. With the witchy lady's skills, they could find it again.

The door burst open, letting in the hallway light. She covered her tightly shut eyes and shouted, "Shut the door!" The bed sank beside her, and she fought the resistance to roll that direction. "Leave me alone." She moaned.

A sharp slap landed on her behind. "Get up!" Santa shouted at her. "Stop acting like it's the end of the world." Using her foot, she pushed at him, causing him to rise from the bed. "The clock is gone and so are my mother and father. Go away and let me grieve."

"This kind of grieving does nothing. You need therapy and the elves need food. Come to the kitchen. You'll feel better as soon as you stir up a batch of cookies. If you want, I'll send Martha on a short sabbatical. You can be alone to grieve while you bake." He tugged on her arm.

Snatching her arm away from his grip, she refused to move. "What I need to do is go back for the clock, but I'm stuck here. I've lost my talisman so I can't go." Her voice quivered, "My sisters don't call. No one cares about me anymore." The tears flowed and she sobbed. No comforting touch or soft words came which caused her to cry more. A flash from the hallway light and the sound of a closing door signaled Santa's exit from the room. She'd never felt so alone.

Time passed as she lay there like a slug, her life signs still going but her mind a blank, until the door flew open and the overhead light was flipped on. "Agh!" she cried out. "Turn it off!" She put her face in the crook of her arm. "It's too bright!"

"Get up!" Martha's voice rang out as she flung the blanket back. "The pity party is over. Time to join the living again." She tugged on Sharon's arm. "I need help in the kitchen. Come on!"

Sharon jerked her arm back and moved to the center of the bed. "Leave me alone. I don't feel good." Curling into a ball, she turned her back on her friend. Solitude was her only comforter. She didn't want Martha interfering with that.

When she heard the door open again, she was relieved Martha got the message and she'd be alone again.

"Come in, backup troop. We have a job to do."

The words jolted Sharon into turning over to see what Martha was talking about. Elwin, Elwina, and Santa joined Martha in her march back to the bedside, looking like ants on their way to a picnic. Martha and Elwina climbed onto the bed and stood over the curled-up Sharon.

Martha bent over her. "You can get out of bed on your own or you can be dragged from it. Your choice. Either way, you're getting out of this bed. Now."

Sharon's breath came quickly, and her heart pounded. Her friends' behavior was strange. They usually supported her in everything, but a mutiny had formed while she mourned. No one understood how she felt deserted by everyone. "Why are you being mean to me?"

Martha supported herself by putting her hands on Sharon's hips and leaning in closer. "You've been locked up in your room all day. You've eaten little and have drunk less. It's the way to bad health, and we're not going to let you go down that road. We're trying to save you because we love you so much. Clarina has an herbal medicine for you to try. She says it'll put the color back in your cheeks."

The words stunned her. All day? It seemed like morning. She blinked away the blindness keeping her bound to her bed. The eyes of the people around her held love and concern. They weren't being mean. They cared. That singular thought was enough to spark a flow of energy as she moved her legs toward the edge of the bed.

Gentle hands helped her to stand beside the bed. Elwin's cheeks reddened and his eyes looked elsewhere as the hem of her nightgown was pulled down to cover her. Her wobbly legs surprised her, unsure why they didn't work as well as they normally did. The helping hands around her got her safely to the rocking chair by the window.

The charger for her phone lay on the table, triggering her need to see if her sisters had called. "I think my cell phone is in the bed somewhere. Can you get it for me?"

Elwin searched through the covers for it, but to no avail. Elwina joined him in the search, and eventually they found the phone under the pillows. Pushing a few buttons, she announced, "It's totally dead. If you have messages, you'll have to recharge your phone before you can see them."

A weight lifted off Sharon. They may have called or left her messages, but her phone was dead and couldn't be reached. She almost let out a cry of joy as she took the phone and plugged it in.

"I can't wait to see if I have messages!" She nearly danced with glee, but after spending so much time in bed, her body wasn't ready for that.

"We'll deal with that later. Right now, you should get dressed," said Santa. His manager side was showing. "I can take it from here," he told the others.

He thanked his three helpers as they left the room. He went to the closet and brought out a pair of sweatpants and a long-sleeved tee shirt. He gingerly helped her dress.

Her ribs were still bruised and hurt as she slipped on the tee shirt but not as much as they hurt before. After straightening her father's necklace on the outside of the shirt, she slipped the pants on. Santa helped her put on thick socks before sliding her feet into her warm slippers. He gave her a brush, and she ran it through her short curly hair.

Feeling more human than she'd felt in a while, a smile moved her face. It was immediately bounced back to her by Santa's smile. He leaned in close to her. "Don't you feel better already?"

Nodding, she sat on the edge of the bed. A growling noise emanated from her midsection, bringing a jolly ho-ho-ho from Santa.

"You must be starved. Let's see what Martha has stirred up for you."

Down the hallway the pair went, drawn to the kitchen by the aroma of ham and sweet potatoes. Her stomach sounded its desires again as she sat by a big plate of the steaming goodness. Like manna from heaven, the meal reinvigorated Sharon, cleared her head, and perked her up. Martha and Elwina sat across the table from her, staring at her every bite. When the last spoon full made its way down her throat, there was still room for dessert.

"I'd love a couple of cookies to follow the delicious meal," she said as she carried her plate to the kitchen. Lifting the lid of the cookie jar, she found it empty. "What? No cookies?"

Elwina stood in the doorway. "You're the cookie baker. There haven't been cookies around here since—" she thought a minute. "Well, since you last baked some."

"That will never do." Sharon began pulling ingredients from the cabinets. "I've neglected my duties long enough. It's time for me to get to work."

The sound of triumph came from her two friends. "I knew my ham and sweet potatoes had medicinal properties," Martha said as she started washing dishes.

Habit took over Sharon's actions, doing things she'd done for years. Each addition of an ingredient felt like dumping troubles into the bowl. With each stir of the spoon, she mixed away her troubles and turned them into something good and delicious. By the time the first sheet full of cookies went into the oven, the cloud around her started lifting. Meaning and purpose had leaked in through the cracks and cheered her. The therapy had worked again.

Seven batches of cookies later, Sharon sat alone at the dinner table enjoying yet another freshly baked cookie. The warm, chewy confection filled her mouth and soul with sweetness. The moment of contentment was interrupted by the approaching sound of buzzing and dinging. Santa rushed in carrying her cell phone.

"This thing came alive when I turned it on. Here," he said, "See what's going on. I suspect your sisters are trying to get a hold of you."

Sharon licked the last of the melted chocolate off her fingers and took her cell phone from him. A list of texts and missed calls scrolled across the screen. Many of them were from elves wishing her a speedy recovery, but some were from her sisters. Her heart leapt at the sign her sisters hadn't forgotten her.

Checking the texts revealed Hannah had been trying to contact her a few hours ago. No recent communication from Essie's had come in. She probably wasn't concerned about her. Pushing the thought out of her head, she said, "Hannah and Headless want to come see us. That surprises me. I didn't think they went anywhere other than Florida."

Sitting beside her, Santa said, "How exciting! We rarely have company."

"I'm supposed to let her know when it's safe to come. It won't take them but a few minutes to get here." She checked Santa's face for an answer.

"How long will they stay?"

Checking the message again, Sharon tried to read between the lines. "Doesn't say. Just says they need to discuss plans for the cottage. I doubt it takes very long. They'll want to be home before their boys come home from school."

His brows were close together as he checked the calendar on his own phone. "Hmm, how about now? I'm not scheduled to inspect our doll workshop until later this afternoon. The elves have questions about the dolls not responding to squeezing."

Sharon typed in her response and sent it. "I wonder what plans they have in mind? Rebuilding? Selling the lot? I'm not sure I could go along with that."

Shrugging, Santa put his phone back in his pocket. "They might want to take a look at the workshop or talk to Godfrey about how to fix the clock."

As they discussed possible reasons for the visit, a chime on Sharon's phone got their attention. It was a response from Hannah. Sharon quickly typed in an answer and sent it back. Grabbing Santa's sleeve, she pulled him along the hallway to his office and pushed him inside. With a whoosh, she shut the French doors and said, "I told them to meet us in here. It's more private." She checked her phone again. "I hope they come quickly. I don't want to set up another time. I can't stand more waiting."

She paced the room, too nervous to sit still. Why did they need to come here? And why was Headless coming too? Curiosity filled her, leaving her jittery.

Santa took her by the shoulders and directed her to the cushioned chair by his desk. "Sit," he said. "You don't want to be in the way when they arrive." The wooden desk chair creaked as he sat in it.

Not many ticks of the clock later, a soft snap filled the room and instantly Hannah and Headless stood there. Sharon jumped up from her seat and rushed to give Hannah a hug. Headless untied the hood and pushed it back from his crooked head. With a swift motion, he righted it before giving Sharon a quick shoulder hug.

"I've got fresh cookies. Let's go to the dining room and I'll make us a snack." She went to the French doors and opened one. "I owe you a treat, Headless. Santa can show you the way while I get things prepared."

Headless didn't move. "Um, I don't eat like normal people so don't worry about me. Besides, I'm not sure we have time."

"No snacks for us," Hannah said as she sniffed the air. "Are those fresh chocolate chip cookies I smell? I'd love to take a couple along when we go."

A giggle of delight escaped Sharon's lips. Pleasing people with food made her day. After making sure the coast was clear, she gave them a tour of her large, aroma-filled kitchen. The multiple wall ovens were still warm from baking and the countertops were still damp from cleaning. Pans and bowls dried in the rack. She was especially proud of the walk-in refrigerator and freezer. "We can't run down the street to the store," she explained. "We have large storage areas for food. We feed over a hundred people every day."

Hannah shook her head. "I don't know how you do it, but it's a good thing you love to cook."

"I have lots of help. Without working together as a team, we couldn't do it." A tinge of guilt pricked her for staying in bed so long.

Headless checked his watch and shuffled his feet. "We need to get back. Can we talk about why we're here?"
Santa led everyone back to his office and made them comfortable. He leaned back in his squeaky chair and said, "What brings you here?"

Headless reached inside his pocket and pulled out a talisman on a cord. Sharon screamed with delight and flashed over to him. "You found my talisman!"

Headless pulled it back away from her. "No, this isn't yours. Mrs. Hagg made one for Santa."

"But—but—"

As if reading her mind, and maybe he could, he quickly added, "She told us each talisman works only for the person

173

for whom it was made. This one is Santa's and will only work for him."

Sharon's happiness flew away like a blown-up balloon let go. "That means mine is gone forever." Her voice held the tears she refused to let go.

Hannah was quickly at her side. "That's part of the reason we came. Mrs. Hagg says she can help us find it. We need your help. Both of you. Once she knows where it is, we can go look for it."

Sharon's balloon of hope filled with a little air. "Really?"

"We have two objectives." Handing the talisman to Santa, Headless went on. "The boys will be gone on an overnight camping trip with friends this weekend. Essie and Easter will come to our house tomorrow. By the way, Mrs. Hagg made him a talisman too. If you come to our house tomorrow afternoon, we'll go over to Mrs. Hagg's house while she consults her—well, whatever she decides to consult to find out where your talisman is located. Using that information, the ladies can try to retrieve it while the men get the clock pieces."

Hannah interjected, "They've opened the area to homeowners so we can go back without fear of being arrested. Again."

The group released their eyerolls, chuckles, and moans at the memory.

Headless brought them back to topic as he turned to Santa. "I trust you have the manpower and skills to put it back together?"

"I do." Santa rubbed his beard and frowned slightly. "Time is what I don't have a lot of. We may not get to it until after my season is over. Our workshop is in full production mode until Christmas Eve."

The matter was put to rest by Hannah. "After Christmas is fine. The main thing is to collect the parts before someone else does and turns them into a recycled lump. Can we count on you coming tomorrow?" She turned to Sharon. "Do you feel up to it?"

Raising her hand to Santa before he could utter his objection, Sharon replied, "We'll be there."

Chapter 19

Hannah

"You shouldn't have told them Easter and Essie were coming," Hannah said to Headless after they returned home. "We haven't asked them yet. I knew Sharon would be easy to persuade to come, but Essie—I never know with her. Don't be surprised if her eternal excuse of being too busy with kids rears its head again."

Taking his hoodie off, he replied, "I plan to appeal to Easter more than Essie. He'll see the value of coming along more than she will." He shook his head. "Essie is a stubborn one."

"I don't intend to talk to her at all if I can help it. I can't forgive her for what she did to me." Hannah checked the time. The boys were at school but would be home soon. If they were going to get this done, they needed to go now. Coming home after the boys got home would only cause more questions she didn't want to answer. "Let's get this over with."

Headless looked out the kitchen window toward the barn. In the distance, Hannah could see their Friesian horses grazing peacefully in the green meadow. Their black coats shone like silver in the sunlight. They were their pets as much as Styx and Shuck. Headless hated selling them, but that's how he supported his family, raising and training horses.

Seeing all was well, Headless acknowledged he was ready to go.

Hannah took out her cell phone and called Essie before noting the time difference. Doing the math, she calculated it was getting late in Germany. "I hope they don't go to bed early." A second later, Essie's impatient and testy voice came on. Hannah felt her chest tighten. She shot a look at Headless who immediately took the phone from her and held it to his ear.

"Hi, Essie," he said more calmly than Hannah could have managed. "Sorry to call so late, but it's imperative we see you and Easter for a few minutes. Can we snap over?"

Essie's voice buzzed through the phone but was indiscernible to Hannah's ear. Rather than try to figure it out, she went back to looking out the kitchen window. The foals kicked and romped around their mothers as they grazed. The pastoral scene calmed her insides as Headless finished the call.

"Ready? They want us to come into their bedroom."

Rolling her eyes, she braced herself for the thunderstorm about to break. "Fine. You handle it. I might choke Essie if you don't."

When the spinning stopped, they were momentarily in blackness before the light came on as Easter came in the doorway. He quickly shut the door behind him and welcomed them to the Bunny home. "I can only offer you a seat on the bed. We don't spend enough time here to have chairs."

Hannah quickly scanned the room. It held a bed and a plain dresser. A door on the side must have led to the master bath or closet. Simplicity marked the décor. She turned back to Easter and said, "We don't plan to stay long enough to sit," Hannah said, wishing Essie had been there to hear it. "I'm sorry for dropping in. Only the urgency brought us here tonight."

The door swung open and Essie marched in. Her lowered brows and unsmiling face portrayed her feelings about the intrusion. She swung the door fast but stopped it short of slamming. A quiet click signaled it was closed.

Stepping closer to Headless, Hannah let him take charge before a cat fight broke out.

His voice was soft, but firm. "The hurricane-damaged areas have been opened to homeowners so they can collect what's left. Tomorrow we want to go get all the pieces of the clock we can find. Santa said he'd take them and try to rebuild it. If we don't go tomorrow, I fear the golden face of the clock will attract real thieves and we'll lose the clock. At this point, I'm hoping it's still there."

Hannah saw Essie's face soften slightly, a good sign considering her previous uncooperative expression. There might be hope their offer would be accepted.

Headless continued. "Beyond the clock, Mrs. Hagg says she can help us find out where Sharon's talisman is, and we can retrieve it." He reached inside his pocket again and pulled out a rock on a cord. He held the dangling rock between him and Easter. "Mrs. Hagg made this one for you, Easter. She told us the talismans we each have work only for whomever it's intended. If we can't find Sharon's, she'll be without one."

Essie crossed her arms. "Too bad for her."

Easter stepped to his wife's side. "Stop it! Have some sympathy for Sharon. You'd be unhappy if you lost yours."

Through gritted teeth, Essie replied, "At least her husband doesn't take her talisman away like she's a two-year-old."

The two glared at each other, and Hannah felt the room get hot on its way to getting hotter. Casting a quick glance at Headless, she knew he felt as uncomfortable as she did.

Headless didn't acknowledge Essie's obvious hostility. He glanced at Hannah and shrugged slightly before saying, "Santa and Sharon will be joining us tomorrow afternoon, and we'd like to have you with us too. We plan to split the chores between us there. But don't feel like you have to come. The invitation is yours to do with as you want." He reached out for Hannah's hand, and his other hand went to the talisman around his neck. He paused, and Hannah waited for an RSVP.

Their response was not immediate. Easter and Essie looked at each other without moving or saying anything. Hannah wondered if they were telecommunicating an answer.

Easter uttered, "We'll be there." He never took his stern eyes off his wife. "Won't we, Essie." His tone left no room for doubt.

"Look," Headless started, "only come if you want—"

Easter broke his stare at Essie. His voice softened and his shoulders relaxed. "This is family business. We'll be there tomorrow afternoon like you said. I'd like to help get the clock."

The cold, stony face on Essie chilled the room. She stared at Easter until he passed near her, and the look of coldness fell on Hannah and left a chill. The feeling was mutual. She didn't like it any better than Essie, but what was left of the clock had to be saved. The men seemed to be on good terms, but could she and Essie put their hostility aside long enough to complete the task? She would try. Once the mission was completed, she'd be rid of Essie.

"I'm happy you'll be there. Meet at our house at two o'clock, our time," Headless said in a brighter tone. The two men shook hands and slapped each other on the back and talked of tools they'd need to dig up the clock.

179

Daring to walk closer to the ice queen, Hannah asked, "What's the problem between you and Easter?" A dagger of a look invoked another question. "Okay, what's the problem between you and me?"

Essie sniffed as her eyebrows shot up. "I'm tired of dealing with family problems. Being nagged about the cottage and the storm. Having to snap here and there anytime anything comes up. It's wearing on the nerves, and I'm tired of it." She stared at her fingers and rubbed her nails with her thumb.

She wasn't the only one tired of all the family drama. Hannah was tired of dealing with Essie's tantrums, Sharon's panics, and being the only one looking after the cottage. That last problem was now moot. With the destruction of the cottage and the clock, the thread holding their relationship together was fraying quickly.

She felt her hand being taken and Headless asking if she was ready to go. Essie looked at her with blank eyes. The sisterhood they'd once felt had been blown away by the storm. One last chore, one last visit to where the cottage once stood, one last goodbye, and the end would come.

She held on to Headless as the spinning began.

When her feet touched the floor of her kitchen, she let out a sound of relief. "Glad I don't live in the Bunnys' house! Did you see how she looked at Easter? I thought she'd bite his head off—oh, sorry, dear. I know you hate that comparison." She got a similar look from Headless as he silently went out the back door.

"Bye, Mom!" Horace yelled out as he ran out the front door with his backpack stuffed full of camping gear. Styx and Shuck followed along after him, barking a chorus of chaos.

"So much for a goodbye kiss," Hannah murmured as she walked out after them. Stowing the last of the camping gear in the back of Huntley's black older-model pickup, Headless added Horace's pack to the pile.

Huntley came up behind her and gave her a quick peck on the cheek. "Don't worry, Mom, he's a dorky sophomore. His mind is a one-track train."

"Watch over him so he doesn't wreck, will you?"
He signaled concurrence as he slung his heavy backpack over his shoulder. "The Outdoor Club leaders will be there to help. See you Sunday night!" Muscular and fit, he trotted out to his pickup and tossed the heavy pack into the back like it was sack of feathers. She admired her handsome sons as they got into the truck. Huntley was the spitting image of his dad, and Horace took more after her. Moreover, they were good sons.

After a few words of last-minute instructions from Headless, the pickup roared to life. With a final wave, Huntley drove his pride-and-joy down the long driveway.
Glancing at the time, Hannah hurried inside to change her clothes into something appropriate for digging and snooping around for Sharon's lost talisman. Jean capris and a maroon tee shirt would conceal her in dark places, if it was necessary to hide from someone. A navy-blue sun shirt would protect her arms from sunburn. Joining her husband in the living room, she clung to him, hoping he'd supply her with some of the patience and fortitude he seemed to have. The day might prove to be a hard one, and she needed all the mental strength she could muster. His strong arms transmitted what she needed.

A snap, followed quickly by another, announced the arrival of the Bunnys. The sight of Easter's skinny white legs below his Bermuda shorts was too silly to keep Hannah's laugh inside. He played along, posing to elicit more laughs. Even Essie laughed along, a relief to Hannah. Maybe the day wouldn't be as bad as she thought it would be.

"I feel overdressed for this mission," Headless remarked in his black slacks and turtleneck shirt. "But trust me, you don't want to see my legs. There are no sunglasses strong enough to save your eyes."

Another snap interrupted the mirth as Sharon and Santa appeared. His even whiter legs were exposed beneath his outfit as well. He let out a hearty ho-ho-ho as he joined Easter in a runway session for the others. Laughter filled the room like sunshine after a gloomy day.

Hannah hated to ruin the joviality, but business was at hand and time was short without the clock to alter it. "Now that we're here, we should go see Mrs. Hagg. She says she can consult her glass to see where Sharon's talisman is." Seeing her guests take hold of their talismans, she assured them it was only a short walk away and no one would see the strange looking group as they went along.

The party went out the front porch, across the large, grassy front yard, and into a heavily wooded area marking the edge of their yard. A faint path led through the maple and walnut trees and dogwood and hawthorn bushes. Birdsong filled the air.

Bringing up the rear of the column, Hannah watched Sharon clinging tightly to Santa as they picked their way through the brush. It was understandable. Hannah would feel as uncomfortable if they were traversing an ice cap.

As the woods got thicker, the birdsong and sunlight disappeared. An owl hooted in the distance, stirring a darker mood in the group. In the thickest part of the woods, the trees stopped suddenly, forming a fortress wall around a crooked little cottage sitting in the middle of a small clearing. The setting looked like something out of a medieval fairy tale. A turkey buzzard sat in a dead tree behind the cottage as if waiting for victims to come to him.

The procession paused at the edge of the woods to survey the scene. To Hannah, it was the house of her friend. Still, she understood why her sisters paused and gawked. She'd done the same the first time she visited Mrs. Hagg.

Headless pressed forward, with the others close on his heels. The Clauses and the Bunnys clung to each other, huddled together as if expecting an attack. Hannah snickered to herself. The vulture was a pet of Mrs. Hagg who hung around because she fed him. She hoped they wouldn't see the snake living under the shed. She fed it too. Most of this was staged to keep strangers away. Mrs. Hagg loved her privacy.

The cottage door swung open as they arrived, and Mrs. Hagg shuffled out. Hannah and Headless warmly greeted their friend and made introductions. Santa and Easter stood unmoving like they were frozen in place, wide-eyed and pale. Essie and Sharon tugged at their husbands. Essie whispered not to be afraid. They greeted the little woman but didn't offer their hands.

"Come in!" Mrs. Hagg called out in a voice like a screech owl. "I've made tea for our visit." She disappeared into the darkness of the cottage.

Headless held the door for the visitors who stood rooted where they stood. Taking the lead, Hannah walked past them and into the cottage. The place smelled funny because of the concoctions being brewed and because of the age of the inhabitant. She walked past the odd cabinet by the door and sat on a stool near the ash-filled fireplace. The others crept inside and gingerly sat on a bench and other stools.

Mrs. Hagg lifted a large kettle from the stove and brought it to the table set with six chipped teacups and saucers. A box of teabags and sweetener sat in the middle by a thick candle providing minimal light. She chatted about how long it had been since she had visitors as she poured hot water into the cups and moved them closer to the intended drinkers. Lastly, she ripped open a package of biscotti and set them in a wooden bowl.

Hannah and Headless helped themselves and sat back with a warm cup of tea watching the others sit like statues with only their eyes moving as they took in the cottage interior. Hannah wanted to slap them, but only hard enough to wake them from their trance. Knowing Mrs. Hagg wouldn't be pleased if her hospitality was rejected, Hannah cleared her throat. A glare at her sisters spurred them into action.

A poke in the side from Essie's elbow brought Easter around. He mumbled a statement of thanks for the new talisman. Santa relaxed a little and offered his gratitude as well.

Mrs. Hagg pulled a stool up next to the table and gave a gap-toothed smile to her guests. "It was no trouble. I'm glad you have talismans." Her eyes fixed on Sharon who seemed to shrink slightly. "Except for you. You lost yours, but it wasn't your fault. You were hurt."

Sharon nodded. "It happened in the storm when I was trying to save our mag—" her eyes widened "—I mean our special clock."

Leaning in a little, Mrs. Hagg stared at Sharon. "You've been sad about losing it. You think you can't go anywhere anymore." She hopped off her stool. "No more worries. I'll find it for you." She shuffled to an ancient china cabinet where numerous crystal balls of many sizes were displayed.

184

Ignoring them, she opened a drawer and pulled out an electronic tablet before returning to her seat. Setting it on the table, she wiped the screen off with her sleeve.

Hannah exchanged glances with Headless. In answer to her unvoiced question, he wiggled his eyebrows. She was confused. Mrs. Hagg's mind might not be working right today. "Uh, Mrs. Hagg..." she began, afraid to hurt her friend's feelings, "...don't you want to get one of your crystal balls instead of this tablet?"

"Oh no. This works as good as one of those things. Besides, this won't roll off the table. I can't tell you how many times I've had to chase a glass ball around my house while trying to see what it was telling me. It's a nuisance." Without turning the device on, she waved her hand over the tablet and muttered something unintelligible.

Hannah had never watched Mrs. Hagg doing her spells before. Forgetting about the others in the room, she sat mesmerized by the hand movements and wondered what words accompanied them. The screen of the tablet shone with mysterious light, growing slightly brighter with each hand wave. Like the billowing of clouds, white images on the screen moved and changed, then went dark.
The six guests leaned in for a closer look, but nothing could be seen.

"Hmm," Mrs. Hagg said, "it must be in a dark place."
Essie offered, "Could be a drawer somewhere."

"Or an evidence bag in a box in the vaults of the police files," Santa said. All eyes turned to him. He shrunk back a little as he explained, "I've seen them on TV."

Mrs. Hagg held up her hand to silence the watchers. Taking the candle, she held it over the tablet. The feeble light seemed to go through the tablet screen and dimly light the place inside the table. With a few candle movements, a cord and a stone came into view. It was the talisman. A collective intake of breath exposed the wonder the watchers felt.

"There it is!" Sharon bounced in her chair.

Amazed at how much was seen in the tablet screen, Hannah asked, "But where is it?"

Moving the candle around so its light exposed other things, writing appeared in the background. Mrs. Hagg moved the candle more and turned the tablet to look in a slightly different direction. Keys and pens were there, along with pens and a tube of lip stain. It looked like the inside of a woman's purse. The light illuminated a transparent business card holder with a pink business card inside. The name on the card was Elvira McKinzor.

Chapter 20

Essie

A pinecone lay in her way. Essie kicked it with the fury she felt inside. "Elvira! I thought we were rid of her," she yelled out to her walking companions. "Last time we saw her, she was disappearing into an avalanche of colored eggs in the back of Howie's car."

A snicker sounded behind her, followed by another. When they walked out of the woods and onto the grassy lawn of the Horseman home, everyone was laughing at the remembered sight of the large woman being stuffed into the backseat of Howie Howard's car in a river of eggs pouring out of it. Santa wiped a tear away as he held his belly with the other hand. With both hands on this head to steady it, Headless bent over in a fit of laughter. The horses in the pasture looked up from their grazing to see what the ruckus was.

By the time they got to the barn, the laughing fit was over, and tears were removed from cheeks. It was time to organize the mission. Essie didn't mind Hannah and Headless heading up the teams. She'd reluctantly come on this crazy trip, but she was glad she had. Mrs. Hagg was an interesting person. Strange, but interesting. Her willingness to help them out despite not knowing who they were was amazing. The bent-over woman seemed to have a heart of gold, like Hannah said, but at the same time, crossing her might be the last mistake anyone made. She wasn't the kind of person anyone would want to get on the bad side of.

While the men gathered a few tools, the sisters stood by the corral fence watching the mares graze as their foals frolicked together. She knew little about the animals but appreciated the beauty of them. "You and Headless raise magnificent horses," Essie remarked.

"People come from all over the world for our horses," Hannah responded. "Headless knows how to handle them and train them. No one does it better." She was working on something on her cell phone and didn't look up.

Sharon tipped her head a little. "I wonder if Santa and the elves could make toy horses to look like them. The flowing manes and long tails would appeal to any child." Pulling out her cell phone, she snapped a few photos.

"Ready for this?" Headless called to them as the men came out of the barn carrying shovels and several feed sacks. "We'll get the clock, and you three get the talisman."

"They're taking the easy job," Sharon murmured as she took more photos of the horses.

Essie couldn't help herself. She revealed out loud their real secret. "They're scared of Elvira."

The three sisters began to titter and snicker as the men approached. When asked what was funny, Sharon continued to snap photos of the horses, and Hannah shook her head saying she was busy with her phone.

Three pairs of masculine eyes rested on Essie. "We were talking about Elvira." The eyes were satisfied and returned to each other's plans for digging the clock out of the sand.

"I've got it!" Hannah cried out, waving her phone in the air. "I know where she lives!"

Amid the praise for Hannah on the use of her minicomputer, Essie wasn't feeling as happy as the others. Part of her had hoped no trace of Elvira would be found, and they wouldn't have to confront her. Still, she understood why Sharon needed her talisman back. They were handy to have around when needing to go somewhere quickly. And they saved a ton of money on airline costs.

All they needed to do was find the lady who had it in her purse and get it without telling her what she had. She knew Elvira couldn't use it but was greedy enough to use it as leverage. Her past fight to own their mother's property was brutal. If her determination to get it said anything about her, it was she'd go to any length to get what she wanted.

"What's our strategy?" she asked the others.

A huddle formed outside the corral, where a stallion was penned. As Headless began telling his plan, the stallion put his large head over the fence and joined them. Headless rubbed his nose and pushed him away which brought a soft nicker for more. More nose rubbing kept the equine interruptions to a minimum.

"Let's go to the cottage and assess the situation. Once we see what needs done, we'll get to work while the ladies go talk to Elvira."

"Talk to that thief?" Hannah yelled. "I want to throw her off a cliff.

Her statement drew raised eyebrows and firm looks. Headless gave her a look that forced her to correct herself.

"Figuratively speaking, of course." After an eyeroll, she went on. "She stole the talisman from the officer who took it from us. The last time I saw it, it was on the table by his computer. I tried to get it, but they put it out of my reach. Too bad they didn't keep it out of her reach."

"But..." Essie began "...how would she know it was something of value? It's a rock on a string to most people. Unless you know what it is, it's like a child's toy or something."

Something switched in Hannah, turning off her nice mood. She gave Essie a sideways glare. "You defending her?"

The air of cooperation was blown away by the sudden cold front coming through. Unsure what brought the accusation on, Essie tried to find something to rebut the accusation as acidly as it was delivered. All she could say was, "No."

Headless leaned over and whispered something in Hannah's ear. She made a face and looked away.

The sweet voice of Sharon neutralized the situation. "She likely saw your talisman around your neck and knew it was something that belonged to us. That's all she needed to know to want it." Making a motion like she was turning a page, she went on, "I appreciate you helping me get my talisman back. It was no fun sitting at home, not knowing what was going on, not being able to go anywhere. It scared me." Her big eyes filled with tears that didn't quite run over. Santa added, "You should have seen her. Curled in a ball on her bed for days. I was afraid she'd never get up." He put his arm around her shoulder and pulled her head to him. He gave her a little peck on her forehead. "I appreciate you all going after the talisman too. It means the world to her."

Hannah's face turned red, and Essie's stomach felt like a knot on a kid's shoelace impossible to untie. The war between her and Hannah was tainting everything. Visions of her unhappy mother rose up in her mind. Guilt piled up inside her. Guilt for not calling her mother back before they lost the cottage and the clock. It was her fault, and she had to make up for it somehow. She owed her sisters that much. She'd get Sharon's talisman back even if she had to help Hannah throw Elvira over a cliff to get it. Figuratively, of course.

190

Hannah must have felt the same way, because with a calm voice she said, "She's malicious enough to take it whether it meant anything or not. She'd use it as a bargaining chip to get our land. From what she said, she's buying up land in the area. Whatever her motivation, we can handle her. We did it before, and we can do it again. She's met her match in the three of us."

The internal and external pep talk boosted Essie's determination. "Let's get this party rolling!"

Minutes later, everyone but the stallion stood in the sandy living room where the cottage once stood. Beyond the remnants of the walls lay debris of wood, rocks, seaweed, and personal belongings blown in from who knew where.

Sharon let out a gasp and threw herself into Santa's arms. It was her first visit back since the storm. Santa's usual jolly demeanor vanished as he paled.

The sight made Essie's heart stop again. She'd never get used to the idea the cottage was gone. She turned to face the direction of the once beautiful beach. It looked different, like someplace she'd never been before. Her head spun a little right before Easter's strong arms steadied her.

"Let's see if the clock is still here." Headless bent down to push the sand away.

A familiar voice came out of nowhere. "It still be here." Slowly the transparent forms of Peg Leg and Rummy Jones appeared near what was left of the chimney. Looking the same as the last time they'd appeared, Essie felt a fondness for the ghostly pirate guards.

Peg Leg leaned against the chimney, with arms crossed and one foot on the wall. "Aye, we run off some scoundrels, but no one else brave enough has come poking around. They say the place is still haunted." He and Rummy Jones let out hearty laughs.

Hannah went over to them. "When did you get here?"

Rummy Jones used his thumb to point at Headless. "Our friend asked ifn we'd stand guard again." He surveyed the surroundings. "Not the place it twas. The storm wiped 'er out but good. With no walls here, we be missing our home."

Essie understood their feelings. If it was depressing to ghosts, it was more so for her and her sisters. The ruins of this happy home were haunting even without ghosts. She wanted to spin her way home, away from everything. Her guilt. Her sisters. Her memories of her mother.

The ghost pirates bid everyone goodbye as they walked toward the beach.

"How will you get back to the lighthouse?" Sharon asked.

They pointed toward the ocean as they walked. As they neared a spot, a dinghy appeared. "It be from the Merribelle," Rummy Jones said. "And I be first mate of her! Ready to shove off, cap'n!"

"Wait!" Hannah called out. "Peg Leg's the captain? I thought it was Captain Fremont's ship."

"Aye," Peg Leg said. "He promoted himself to owner and made me the temporary captain of his ship until he decides to go to sea again. He be very happy hanging out with his true love Adella McPhee, but I hear she runs a taut ship. He may need to find his sea legs again." The two ghosts let out a chuckle as they went out to their dinghy sitting at the edge of the surf on the shore.

Peg Leg stood on one side of the boat and Rummy Jones on the other. A quick push and Peg Leg jumped inside. Rummy Jones pushed a few more steps before climbing inside. The dinghy bounced and pitched in the surf as Rummy Jones used the oars to pull them farther out into the water. With a last salute from Peg Leg, they faded out of sight.

Odd as it seemed, their ghostly presence had comforted Essie. It took her thoughts away from the dreariness of loss and back to the mission yet to be accomplished. If those two ghosts left their comfortable existence to do a favor for them, it was the least she could do to help her sisters recover a valued trinket.

Chapter 21

Sharon

The sand flew up out of the hole the men were digging and got into Sharon's shoes as she watched. The face of the clock was uncovered, and the excavators were looking for what lay below it. More videotapes, dishes from the kitchen, and more of the coffee table appeared out of their sandy graves.

The night the clock fell on her was replaying itself in her head. Over and over again. She tried to hold the clock upright, but it was too heavy. It pushed her down and pinned her to the floor as the water came inside the cottage. The roar of the wind, the clock falling, the water covering her face, the weight of the clock holding her down, the lack of air, the weight lifting off, and her first breath. She saw it again in her mind. Headless had saved her, and she was eternally grateful to him for risking his life for her.

The men were on their knees pushing sand away from the floor of the cottage. Amid the videotapes and wood debris, parts of the clock appeared in the sand. Carefully pulling each piece out, it was gingerly cleaned and put into the sack for transport to the workshop. As one feed sack was filled, another one was pulled out of the stack.

Essie and Sharon collected several videotapes and shoved them inside a bag while Hannah walked along the water's reach. Reshaped and covered with ocean debris, the beach they'd grown up playing on was unrecognizable. It was no longer her mother's beach.

As interesting as this was, Sharon's heart lay somewhere else. It was wondering where Elvira and her talisman were. The men were handling this chore. It was time for the ladies to do theirs.

"Don't you think it's time we go find Elvira?" she shouted so Hannah could hear her. Her voice wavered a little, though she tried to keep the emotion out of it. A feeling of urgency was releasing a pang of panic, but she easily pushed it away. Clarina's herbal mix seemed to be working.

Headless straightened up and wiped his brow. "We have this handled. Go do what you need to do. We'll meet you back at our house when you're done."

Santa tried to get off his knees, but the sand kept moving under him. Sharon hurried over and helped him up. "I'm not used to sand in my shorts," he said wiping sand off his bare legs. "It's a little…uncomfortable."

"A quick dip in the water will get rid of some of it," Hannah offered as she walked up. "But being wet will make sand stick more to the wet parts of you. Be careful until you dry."

Easter wiped his brow and put his hat back on. "There's nothing dry in this humidity." He stretched his muscles. "This sand doesn't weigh much but it's hard to work in."

Taking his head off its brace, Headless held it in the crook of his arm while he wiped it with his bandana. "We can handle our part. You should go find Elvira and see what's in her purse."

Sharon's heart beat a little faster. "Yes, let's go." The sooner she had her talisman back, the sooner things would get back to normal. Everything and everyone would be back where they belonged.

Santa wished good luck to Sharon. Essie gave her husband a pat on the back before joining Hannah who was looking at her phone. Headless gave them a thumbs up. Sharon's excitement grew as she joined her sisters.

"Her office is close to downtown. With the damage, her office may not be open. There are probably very few real estate sales going on at the moment."

Sharon, usually more of a follower, blurted out, "Let's start there." She bounced slightly with nervous energy.

Hannah looked at her with amused eyes before she went back to the phone's display. "If she's not there, I found an address for her, but it's inside a gated community."

Essie clutched her chest. "I'm not ready for more law enforcement dealings."

"You got your passport?"

Pulling up her shirt, she showed a travel pouch. "I won't come here without it again."

Hannah cocked her head. "One more thing before we go. No more desertions. If we get caught, we're in it together. Right?"

Seeing Essie's trembling hands put her shirt back in place made Sharon's breathing speed up. She didn't have a passport or driver's license, and it was too late to get one now. If they got caught, she'd be the one arrested as an illegal alien. No identification and no talisman to make a quick getaway.

No matter. The desire to get her talisman was too strong to resist. She wouldn't voice her concerns but would instead hope for the best. If things got bad, she'd throw herself on the nearest sister and hang on with all her might. She might get flung into the ocean or another dimension during the spinning, but it was the best escape plan. Her hands started to tremble in sync with Essie's.

Hannah took her talisman off from around her neck and said, "Let's go together so we end up in the same place. Take hold."

With each sister holding onto the cord, Hannah recited the chant and snap! they stood in an alley behind a strip mall. The sound of traffic came around the end of the building, signaling a busy street on the other side. A disheveled residential area stretched out beyond the downed privacy fence running the length of the alley.

A quick look around revealed no one else was in the vicinity. Their arrival was unseen other than a gray cat staring at them from underneath the garbage bin. Walking around the end of the long building, they saw a few cars in the parking lot. One nail care store was still boarded up. One storefront owner was busy removing the plywood from his windows. The other businesses had open doors and glass windows exposed.

Two linemen's bucket trucks drove by as the sisters stood there. The electricity must have been restored to this section of the town. An insurance office, a liquor store, and a coffee shop had open signs in the window.

On the far end of the strip mall was a large sign reading Elvira's Excellent Estates. Seeing the target of their visit, they hurried down the sidewalk. Looking through the large plate glass window with nail holes around the sashing, the sisters saw two young, good-looking men staring at computer screens.

Sharon's heart jumped. "They're open! Let's go get my talisman." She marched through the doors like a queen and her entourage. The men gawked at her as she sashayed to the nearest desk and leaned over it. "Tell Elvira the daughters of the crazy woman would like to see her."

Eyebrows shot up as the two men looked at each other. One shrugged and the other repeated, "Daughters of the crazy woman?"

"She knows who we are," Sharon said, standing up straight. The quest to get her talisman back was nearly at an end, and she felt new confidence. This time Elvira wouldn't intimidate her.

The man picked up the phone and punched in a few numbers. "Um, the daughters of the crazy woman are here to see you," he said as if he were tiptoeing on glass. His eyes darted around, then to the three ladies standing in front of his desk. "Okay." He hung up and announced, "She's not here. Take a card and send her an email." He held out one of her sickly pink business cards.

Her breath came quickly, but it wasn't from fear. Heat surged through Sharon. Feeling emboldened by the surge of ire, she took the card and flicked it back at him. A hallway to the side led to other offices and knowing Elvira's type, hers would be the largest and most ornate. Like a shot out of a canon, she flew down the hallway. Her entourage and the young men provided background noise as she went toward a door with the detested name on it. They tried to pull her back, but she had none of it. She swung the door open and marched into an empty office.

This shrine to the queen of awful taste almost triggered Sharon's gag reflex. The office's interior decorating centered on Elvira's favorite colors. The wall behind her massive white desk was painted black and was decorated with multiple certificates in hot pink frames surrounding a giant aerial photo of Sarasota with gold stars scattered across it. Pink and white cloth flowers framed a photo of Elvira on the mezzanine behind the desk. The other walls were painted the same sick pink on her business cards and were covered with photos of her with what was assumed were her many properties. Papers were scattered across the top of the desk with several sheets on the floor beside it. A coat rack was tipped over against the wall, like someone had grabbed a coat and hurried out. A large picture window looked out at the parking lot and the street.

"See," on the of young men said, "I told you she wasn't here."

Even as he said the words, the backside of Elvira running toward an SUV was framed in the large window. She lost one shoe, paused, then went on without it. Throwing her large bejeweled bag into the vehicle, she crawled in and started the engine. The squealing tires sounded her speed like the doppler effect.

"Come on, girls!" Sharon went through the backdoor of Elvira's office and ran out of the building. As the door slammed behind them and locked, she said, "Get your talisman, Hannah. Let's go get her!"

"But—but—" Hanna pulled it over her head. "—we don't know where she's going."

"Doesn't matter," Sharon said as she grabbed one side of the talisman. "Get hold, Essie! Hannah, say the words and I'll fill in the destination."

"PopmybubbleI'mintroubletakemethereonthedouble."

"Back of Elvira's SUV!" she yelled.

Any protests her sisters had were swallowed by the spinning and the sudden shift as they found themselves horizontal in the cargo area of a wildly driven SUV. Sharon put her hand over her mouth to keep from crying out as they turned a corner sharply, throwing the three women in a heap against one side. She was relieved to know the other two kept their silence as well. She should have thought about the decision more, but no matter. Another corner taken at high speed, and they rolled to the other side of the vehicle.

Her sisters probably thought this was a dumb idea, but Sharon was determined to get her talisman back. Without it, she'd be stuck away from her sisters, Sam, and anywhere else she wanted to go easily.

The SUV gradually slowed and drove more sensibly, making it more comfortable for the sisters crammed in the back of the SUV. Untangling themselves, the ride became more comfortable and less tense.

"Now what?" Essie said in a barely audible whisper. Sharon didn't know. Her act had been one of desperation, not of planning the next move. No quick answer came, but an answer presented itself.

The calmer ride made it easier to hear what Elvira was muttering to herself. She was scared, that was plain. They heard her tell her Bluetooth connection to call Howie. Shortly, a familiar voice sounded out.

"Whatcha need, El?" His tone was less than friendly.

"They're back, Howie. The girls of that crazy woman. They came to my office today."

"What did they want?"

Elvira honked at someone and swerved before speeding around a corner, making the sisters roll to the other side of the cargo area. "I didn't stick around long enough to find out."

"Why not? They may want to sell their property. If what I've seen is any indication, that rattrap of a cottage is gone. We could get it for a song."

Sharon turned her head to see what her sisters were thinking. One pair of eyes rolled and the other had fire in them. Same as her. Essie held up her talisman and signed to take hold. Hannah did, but Sharon shook her head. This was as close as she'd be in getting her talisman back and she wasn't leaving until she had it. Hannah shook her finger at her, but she shook her head again. She tried to push their hands away, but they resisted.

"I'm not sure the property is worth it. Remember what happened last time we dealt with them. You were out of commission for months."

Hands came away from the talisman.

Howie growled. "I'll never forget it. My only revenge is getting the property from them and making millions. I dream of that every night."

Essie returned the talisman around her neck. Feeling vindicated for staying, Sharon waited for more revelations.

"Go back," the man said, "and ask them if they're ready to sell. Offer them the minimum. We can go up a little, but we won't go far. From what I've seen of the damage, there's little left there. Our offer will be more than they can get anywhere else."

The SUV slowed and made a U-turn. Satisfied with knowing what they knew, Sharon signed she was ready to go. The three sisters took hold of Essie's talisman and left their uncomfortable ride.

Chapter 22

Hannah

A chant, a spin, and a snap had the three inside Elvira's ornate office. Hannah didn't know whether to hit Sharon or hug her. Her bold move to take them to the back of the SUV had garnered valuable information, but if they'd been discovered there, they'd be in jail on charges of…of…something. She couldn't think of a law against hitching a ride with someone, but it didn't matter. Sharon shouldn't have done it.

Recklessness from her mildest sister was shocking. And unexpected. Perhaps she'd underestimated what Sharon was capable of or would do if determined enough. And she did it without a paper bag over her face.

Creeping to the office door, Essie closed and locked it. Her face was red and stern. "Sharon, don't you EVER do that again!" she said in a contralto voice. She smoothed her hair and her clothes and took a breath. "Putting us in the back of her van is absolutely the craziest thing you've ever done. I'd never speak to you again except, well, I hate to admit it, being there gave us a clue about their evil plotting against us. Those two thieves never give up."

"Nor do I," Sharon said with surprising firmness. "I want my talisman, and I'll wrestle her for it if I have to. Or maybe we can find a cliff."

Hannah couldn't believe her ears. This timid, panic-stricken sister of hers was a pit bull about the talisman. The new Sharon deserved encouragement, although too much might make her overconfident.

A titter of laughter erupted out of Hannah. "Can you imagine what Elvira would have done if she'd caught us in the back? She might have wet herself." Her laughter made her sisters shush her. She put her hand over her mouth to stifle it.

The humor was lost on Essie who retained her sour look. "Or wrecked. We could have been killed! It's nothing to laugh at. How would Easter explain it to my kids?

Sitting in one of the chairs in front of the desk, Sharon told her," Don't be such a pessimist, Essie. We didn't wreck, and we didn't get caught. Thanks to the ride, we know what they're planning to do. When she gets here, we can thwart those plans in a hurry."

Hannah paced around the office. She agreed more with Sharon than Essie. The advantage was theirs as far as the property was concerned, but they weren't any closer to getting the talisman back. They hadn't planned a way to get it out of her purse.

When the phone rang, they stared at it as if wanting it to answer itself. It rang twice and stopped. The men out front must have answered it and quiet returned to the pink office.

The silver SUV pulled into a parking space outside the large window. Elvira pulled the visor down and checked her lipstick, and pushed it back up. Getting her large bag, she climbed out of the tall vehicle. She jiggled and danced as she pulled clothes out of places where they didn't belong and put them where they did.

Her chubby toes peeked out of the end of one of her sandals as she looked around for the missing one. She walked to the back of her vehicle and returned carrying a matching sandal looking like flattened roadkill. Her face scrunched in anger as she stomped her bare foot and her sandaled foot as she went toward the side entrance door.

Sharon sat up in her seat in front of the desk while Essie sat in the other. Hannah stood behind them, arms crossed like she was her sisters' bodyguard. Hannah decided to let Sharon run the show since it was her crusade. She was proud of her sister's calm but determined demeanor. Just then, Sharon put her hand over her face like she did when a panic attack was coming. Hannah reached down and gave her shoulder a squeeze.

Sounds came from the locked door and it swung open as Elvira walked in. Her mouth fell open, and her face went white under her makeup. For an instant, Hannah was worried she'd turn and run, but Elvira composed herself and came in. Her bag landed on her desk with a loud thud.

Hannah couldn't help but stare at the bag. If Mrs. Hagg was right, all they needed to do was get Elvira out of the room, leaving them free to look inside. The talisman was there. Within their reach. So close it was almost calling to her. Once they found it, it was home sweet home.

Elvira's desk chair squeaked when she leaned back in it. "I see you waited for me to come back." Elvira entwined her fingers.

The doorknob behind Hannah rattled as someone tried to get in. The sound of a key unlocking it came through before it flew open as one of the men from the front came in. He let out an utterance of surprise and sidestepped the three women sitting in front of his boss's desk. "Um, how did you ladies get in here? You weren't here a little bit ago." His eyes went between Elvira and the sisters. "I've been at my desk the whole time. How did you get in here?"

Her eyes never left the sisters as Elvira told him, "They own a haunted house. They are creepy people who you're better off not knowing. Get out of here, Cole."

Dropping a file on her desk, he sidestepped them again as he left.

Sharon drummed her fingers on the chair's arm as she stared at Elvira. "Sorry we scared you off earlier."

Elvira let out a nervous laugh and played with her rings. "I wasn't scared. I—I—My pharmacy called and had my order ready." She rearranged two pens on her desk as she regained her composure. "No matter. What brings you to my office? Ready to sell your land?"

Sharon leaned forward. "All I want is what's mine. You have it in your purse. A small necklace made of a rock on a cord. It was a gift, and I want it back."

Elvira sat back. Her eyes narrowed as she said, "What makes you think I have it?"

Hannah stepped to the side of her desk, forcing Elvira to swivel and look her way. "It was on the table in the tent where I was being held by the National Guard. I'm sure you remember seeing it. You were there, and the necklace was gone after you left. Doesn't take many brains to figure out who has it." When sweat broke out on Elvira's top lip, Hanna knew they were cracking the tough exterior. She leaned closer. "Just give us the necklace, and we're out of your life for good."

Elvira jumped out of her chair and paced behind the desk. "You can't prove I took it."

Sharon stood up. "Yes, we can, but you wouldn't like it. You know we have supernatural friends who are good at peering into purses and seeing what's next to your lipstick and business cards. And as easy as that, I found my necklace. In your purse." She slowly sat again. "I'm not leaving here until I get it. And I'm prepared to call Headless and his friends to make sure."

Stopping her movements, she leaned across her desk. "Don't threaten me."

Standing up and facing her, Sharon said sweetly, "It's not a threat. It's a warning that I'll do what I have to do to get my necklace back."

With shaking hands, Elvira lifted her bag and dumped its contents into a small mountain on her desk. The sisters stood and hovered over the pile. With a swift motion, Elvira snatched the cord and held the talisman in the air by her head. It swung beside her ear, out of reach of the sisters.

"It must be valuable for you to go to all this trouble to get it." She stroked the stone, then glared at Sharon. "Does it have some sort of magic?"

Sharon remained unmoving. "None for you."

A sinister chuckle came from Elvira. "I'll give it to you, but you must give me something in return. Your property. It's worth nothing to you now. Sell it to me. I'll give you more for it than anyone else will." Her eyes darted between the three sisters, looking and searching.

Like her sisters, Hannah stood stone-still. They hadn't discussed what they'd do with the property since the cottage was gone, but she was certain of one thing: none of them would agree to sell it to Elvira. Not even for the million dollars they offered last time they met. No matter what her sisters wanted, she'd hold out to do something else with it.

"Give me the talisman," Sharon began, "and we'll seriously consider your offer. No necklace, no consideration at all."

Elvira folded the cord and rock in her hand. "Not good enough. You sell. You get your necklace. If you wait in the outer office, I'll tell my boys to prepare the sale papers. Once they're signed. I'll give you the necklace." She looked at it and felt of the stone. "What's so special about this?

Something supernatural?" Holding it closer, she added, "It's ugly."

A snap sounded from the corner of the room. All eyes looked toward the noise and saw Headless, head under his arm, standing there. Beside him stood the shriveled form of Mrs. Hagg. With a kick, he slammed the office door shut and reached over to lock it. He came over to the big white desk and put his head on it. His hands pressed together as his knuckles cracked.

Elvira's eyes couldn't have been any larger without them popping out. She pointed a shaky finger at him. "It's you again! You're not real! You're a dream!" Pointing at Mrs. Hagg, she howled, "And you brought an awful little creature with you!" She shut her eyes tight as if a bright light was shining in them. "It's just a dream. It's just a dream. It's just a dream."

Mrs. Hagg wobbled her way beside Elvira and gave a cackling laugh. "It's not a dream. It's your worst nightmare if you don't hand over the necklace. I gave it to Sharon, and I want her to have it back." Hooking the top of her cane over Elvira's wrist, she pulled on her hand holding the necklace. She unfolded the stiff fingers and lifted the talisman out of it. With a glowing snaggle-toothed grin, she handed the talisman to Sharon.

Headless picked up his head and held it by her ear. "Don't ever bother my girls again, or I will come back and make sure you know this is not a dream."

Elvira never opened her eyes or stopped repeating her mantra as the four of them whispered the chant and went home.

Chapter 23

Essie

Essie's legs were weak when they landed in Hannah's living room. Stumbling, she made her way to the sofa and plopped down. The ride in the back of the SUV and the confrontation with Elvira had drained her of strength. Someday their adventure might be funny, but not today.

Her sisters must have felt the same. Both fell on the sofa beside her. Sharon called for a paper bag but having none handy, she put a decorative pillow over her mouth and nose. The action surprised Essie. The last few hours, mild-mannered Sharon had been a tower of strength, but she had returned to her normal self, like Superman transforming back into Clark Kent.

Flipping the pillow away, Sharon let out a cry of victory as she held the talisman before her face. The stone swung, drawing her shining eyes back and forth with it. "The cord is broken, but I can fix it. It's back where it belongs." Jumping up, her chubby legs carried her around the room as she danced, hugging everyone there, even Mrs. Hagg.

A big question remained, and Essie had to know the answer. "Headless, how did you know we needed help with Elvira?"

The tall man secured his head to its rightful position after a vigorous hug from Sharon. "Mrs. Hagg told me things weren't going smoothly, and you might need assistance."

Mrs. Hagg cocked her head and crossed her arms. "No one steals my gifts without consequences. She deserved more than a good scare, but Headless said I had to hold back." Giving a wink, she let out a high-pitched cackle. "That woman is not a nice person. And she's hideous!"

Sitting in a recliner, Hannah offered, "Thank you for watching us. We weren't going to leave without the talisman, but without your help, it would have taken longer to get it away from her."

"Just how much do you watch people?" Essie asked as visions of her and Easter and their children ran through her head. Being spied upon through social media was not quite as disturbing as being spied up on by a strange little woman.

Mrs. Hagg sat on the ottoman which accommodated her short stature nicely. "I see only what I choose to see. When a situation involves trouble for my friends, I keep watch close." Lacing her long, gnarled fingers together, she gave a crooked smile to Hannah who returned the same.

Sharon took a place on the sofa, a little pale and sweaty from her celebrating. Patting Sharon's knee, Essie remarked, "You amazed me today. You handled Elvira like a pro. And snapping us to the back of her SUV, that was quick thinking."

"Wildest ride I've ever been on," Hannah said as she got up.

Headless grabbed her arm to stop her from leaving. "Wait. What's this about a wild ride?"

"Let Sharon tell it," Hannah said as she went into the kitchen. "I'll make iced tea and sandwiches for us all. By the way, where's Santa and Easter?"

"In the barn with Godfrey," Headless said loudly enough so Hannah could hear.

The name perked up Sharon. "Godfrey's here already?"

"He brought a small, one-reindeer sleigh. Santa said he flew below the radar, but out of sight. I'm not sure how that's possible, but I don't ask questions."

Clapping her hands together, Sharon declared, "Godfrey is our elf who can repair anything. He used to repair clocks, but he had to expand his repair skills when clocks went out of vogue. If anyone can put Father's clock back together, Godfrey can." Sharon got up from the sofa, teetered slightly, and made her way toward the back door. "I guess all that excitement was too much for me."

Headless was quickly at her side. "You may not be fully recovered from your accident. Let me help you out to the barn. I want to hear about this wild ride." The two of them made their way through the kitchen and out the back door.

Essie pulled herself off the sofa and ambled into the kitchen. Hannah was pulling sandwich makings out of the refrigerator. Paper plates were already out, waiting to be filled. Her offer to help was brushed aside. She sat at the table and watched the lunch preparations. Easter would hear about their adventures from Sharon and interrogate her about them later.

Her body cried out for rest. The hours she'd gone through felt like they'd each been a day long. If they got the clock working, she'd ask Hannah to set it to five o'clock so she could take a long nap before going home. With time on the outside slowed down, she could go home rested rather than exhausted.

"Essie, take this tablecloth and put it over our picnic table out back." She held out a neatly folded red-and-white gingham cloth and a bucket with cleaning supplies in it.

Grateful for an errand to keep her from dozing in a chair, Essie took it and went out the back door. A metal picnic table sat under a large oak tree about halfway between the house and the barn. From there, the horse pasture was in full view which added a sense of peace to the environment. The bucket had water, soap, and a long-handled brush which made cleaning the table off an easy chore. The table soon air dried, and the tablecloth went on the clean surface.

Hannah came out with a tray loaded with food and eating utensils. She gave them to Essie to distribute around the table while she went back for cups and drinks. Before she went in the house, she rang a bell hanging on one of the patio cover's posts. The sound rebounded around the backyard and out to the barn. By the time Hannah returned, the five people from the barn were headed to the picnic.

The three men made the elf Godfrey seem even smaller. His face reminded Essie of a picture of Rumpelstiltskin she'd seen in a children's book somewhere. His overlarge nose bent over his upper lip, and his white Lincoln beard hung across the front of his shirt like a bib. He and Easter were engaged in conversation, probably about their enjoyment of fixing broken things.

As everyone took their places, Godfrey chose a seat beside Mrs. Hagg. The two were about the same size and were soon lost in conversation.

Hannah came out from the house with two pitchers and cups on a tray. The group from the barn got to the picnic table and randomly took seats. Shuck and Styx sat behind Headless, ears perked up as the food was passed around. Easter sat beside Essie and leaned over and whispered he was glad she hadn't gotten arrested again. Godfrey was introduced to Hannah and Essie before Santa said grace.

The simple meal tasted as good as any five-star restaurant to the hungry people. Chatter about their adventure filled the air as they ate. Finishing her sandwich, Sharon said she regretted not bringing a few of her cookies along when she came. Easter offered to pay for pizza if the clock wasn't fixed by suppertime. He gave Essie a wink.

Godfrey wiped his mouth on his napkin. "No worries. The clock is almost back together. A few more springs and tweaks and she should be good as new."

Sharon clapped her hands. "Godfrey, you are the best! I thought we'd never have the clock running again. You're truly a miracle worker."

He shook his head. "No miracles. Just cleaning and putting things back where they belong. It was missing many of the little pieces, but thanks to my toolbox, I had springs and coils to fit. Good thing they found the mainspring, gear train, and escapement, otherwise it would have been a lost cause."

Santa asked for more salad. "The case is gone, but Headless rigged a box that holds the workings well enough for the clock to operate."

Checking her watch, Essie calculated the time at her house. The children might need help with their homework before suppertime. What would they have for supper? She shut her eyes and tried to remember what leftovers were in the refrigerator. They were old enough to cook their own supper, but she preferred to be there to make sure they made something healthy. The sooner they knew if the clock worked, the faster her life would get back to normal. "How much longer before we see a demonstration of it?"

Godfrey wiped his mouth again and pushed his plate away. "Half hour maybe. Headless said we should try it in the house."

To encourage them to hurry, Essie took Easter's plate as soon as he picked up the last bite and put it with her empty plate. The action had the desired effect as people finished and returned to their workplaces. Before Easter left, Essie gave him the look, hoping he'd read her mind about hurrying along.

212

The sisters gathered the leftovers, scraps the dogs didn't eat, and dirty dishes and hauled them back to the house. Mrs. Hagg bid them all goodbye and left to go home. They had barely finished cleaning the kitchen when the men came from the barn bearing the repaired clock.

Looking nothing like their mother's clock other than the face, Easter and Godfrey put the repaired timepiece on the edge of the kitchen table. The hands were set to nine-fifteen as directed by Sharon but were moved to three o'clock for testing. If it worked, they would enjoy a visit with their mother for twenty-four hours.

Godfrey attached the pendulum and gave it a push. A soft ticking sound filled the room and spread smiles all around. The smiles stayed as the seconds ticked by. Santa congratulated Godfrey for a job well done, and Headless dittoed the sentiment.

Everyone was happy and smiling except the sisters. Something was wrong. The clock worked. Their mother's clock had never worked. It stayed at three o'clock even when it ticked as the pendulum moved. They waited to see if the pendulum stopped, but it kept swinging as the second hand went around and moved the minute hand to three-oh-one, three-oh-two, three-oh-three. Something was wrong. Godfrey had fixed the clock, but he hadn't restored the clock.

Disappointment swelled in Essie's throat as she watched the clock move to three-ten. The clock was ruined forever, taking with it her mother and father. Tears formed in her eyes like they did in Sharon and Hannah's eyes.

The smiles in the room faded as the men noticed the tears rolling. "But it's working!" Godfrey's tone plead with them to not cry. "Isn't that what you wanted?"

Sharon wiped her face on Santa's offered handkerchief before she went to him and gave him a hug. "Of course, it is. Thank you. It's just that—" her voice gave way.

Essie finished it. "It's just that we thought all hope was gone, and you have it working. We're sorry we're crying but you know how sentimental women are."

Godfrey seemed satisfied with their answer and a smile returned to his face. Santa went to him and put his arm around his shoulders. "We've kept you here long enough. I'll go hook up the work sleigh for you so you can head home."

The men went out to the barn, leaving the sisters to weep freely. Essie went to the sofa and leaned against the arm. The load of failure lay on her. She'd neglected to call their mother back for the last time. She'd ignored Hannah's pleas for help in boarding up the cottage before the storm. She'd failed her sisters in every way, and now they had nothing except a sandy piece of worthless land and a working grandfather clock. Her hand went around her neck, wanting to find her talisman to make a quick escape. Instead her hand found the metal chain of the necklace her father left for her after his last visit. She pulled it out from under her blouse and held it tightly in her hand.

"I'm sorry, Father," she whimpered as her tears wetted her cheeks.

Chapter 24

Sharon

Her chest was tight, and her breath hardly came. Her head began to spin like it was going off with the talisman on its own. Through her wavy vision, she saw a recliner and headed for it before she fainted. Falling into its open arms, she tried to steady herself, but the incessant ticking of the clock felt like darts being thrown at her.

Her fingers went into her ears to block the sound. "Stop the ticking!"

Curled into a ball, she lay in the chair waiting to see what the next second brought. After a while, she opened one eye. The room seemed quiet, other than the sniffles and quiet weeping of her sisters. Uncurling, she looked at the table where the repulsive contraption sat silent.

She couldn't take her eyes off it. The face of the clock was the same familiar one she'd grown up with, but it read three-twelve. Her mother's clock had never read three-twelve. This couldn't possibly be her mother's clock. They'd dug up someone else's clock. Her heart sank as she realized the face of it was exactly like her mother's clock, but it was coincidental. If it was her mother's clock, the magic should still be there.

She sat up straighter. To know for certain, they needed to run a test. If Essie was willing, they'd set the clock to twelve and see if their father appeared like he had twice in the past. Only then would they know whether the clock was real or not. But her sisters would have to agree to the experiment since it involved calling him back. Would they let her wait for him this time?

Essie was draped over the arm of the sofa, her shoulders moving as she silently wept. Hannah sat on the other end stone-faced and staring into space. Sharon sat a while longer. Her chest loosened as a plan of action came together. Her head cleared more.

"Girls, I don't think this is our mother's clock, but to be sure, I have a proposition. Let's set it to twelve o'clock and see if Father comes back. If he does, then it is her clock. If he doesn't, it's not."

Still stone-faced, Hannah stared at her. Essie barely moved, but her shoulders quit shaking.

Wanting to break the anguish holding them in its grip, Sharon continued. "I know Father's a busy man, but I don't think he'd mind us calling. He'll want to know about Mother's cottage and the clock. I say we call Father and see what happens."

Essie turned to face her, puffy eyes and all. "That's a great idea. He'll be glad we called him even though he might be busy."

Hannah finally came to life. "I feel like Sharon does. If he comes, he can put the clock back the way it was. Make it work like it's supposed to. Let's find out and get this over with. We've waited long enough."

Essie's shoulders straightened and her red eyes perked up. "Let me set the clock. A lot of what's happened was my fault. I'll have to explain to Father what I've done." With the movements of a sloth, she made her way to stand in front of the silent clock. She put the hands to twelve. Giving the pendulum a gentle push, the three sisters stood together as the ticking started. The seconds kept ticking. And kept ticking. The minute hand moved to the one and the seconds kept ticking. When the minute hand reached three, Sharon knew it was over. The magic had left the clock.

As Essie slumped to the floor, Sharon joined her, followed by Hannah. The three women in a row on the floor, the clock still ticking off the seconds. Hannah reached up and grabbed the pendulum to still it.

Anger swelled inside Sharon. This clock had betrayed her. She'd almost lost her life trying to protect it from the storm. Hannah had been arrested trying to protect it. They'd rescued it from its sandy grave and put it back together. But the ungrateful timepiece refused to function properly.

She leaned closer to it and saw where the pendulum hooked into the clock workings. Unhooking it from its place, she took it off. Rising, she held it like a club in her hand. With a mighty whack, she hit the clock with the pendulum. A metallic twang filled the room. In an instant, Essie was at her side reaching for the pendulum. With a grunt of effort like a tennis player, she swung the pendulum and struck the face of it, causing a dent. The deformed pendulum went next to Hannah who gave it another mighty wallop, knocking the second hand off the face. A shout of triumph went up.

The back door opened, and the three husbands came in. "What's going on it here?" Headless asked. Seeing the pendulum in Hannah's hand, he added, "Doesn't the clock work?"

"No, it doesn't," Sharon told them. "It's either not Mother's clock or Godfrey took the magic out of it."

Santa frowned. "Godfrey is a good man! He—"

Sharon held up her hand. "I didn't mean he did it on purpose. He repaired the clock, but it doesn't work like it used to. We set it to three o'clock to call Mother, but she didn't appear. We set it at twelve to call Father, but he didn't come. The clock is dead."

217

Easter pushed his cap back and scratched his head. "You mean after our trouble to get it back here, it doesn't work? Did we miss something in the sand?"

"No," Headless said, "we went through the sand with a fine-tooth comb. If we didn't find the magic component, it wasn't there."

Hannah banged the clock with the pendulum again, bending it as she did. Headless took the pendulum away from her. "Let's take this back to the barn and get you three hammers. If you want to beat this thing to pieces, don't do it on the kitchen table." He picked up the contraption and carried it outside to the edge of the patio. "Wait here," he told them. Returning in a few minutes, he had three hammers to hand out to anyone wanting to take a swing at the worthless clock.

Frustrations and anger gave strength to the sisters as they pounded the clock into scrap metal. It was no less than it deserved. When strength and breath failed them, the sisters threw the hammers down and declared victory over their foe. Rarely resorting to such destructive behavior, Sharon felt restored and whole again, having shown the clock how she felt about it. She wouldn't be fooled by it again.

As the men cleaned up the metallic mess, the sisters returned to the living room. They took their places on either end of the sofa and Sharon in the recliner. She pulled out the necklace her father had left her on his last visit. "This is all we have left of our parents. Memories and this necklace."

"And a few sand-filled videotapes," Hannah added as she pulled out her necklace. "Mother's plan to reconcile us worked, but we let her down in the end."

Essie pulled out her necklace and rubbed it like a worry stone. She stood up and yelled, "Go ahead and say it. I, yes, I..." she pounded her chest "...let her down. I didn't call her back when I should have, and I'm the reason we won't see her again. Go ahead and say it. It's my fault!" Her face contorted right before she covered it with her hands. Her sobbing filled the room.

Closing her eyes, Sharon looked deep inside herself. She did blame Essie, but she didn't deserve all the blame. They'd all been busy. They'd all ignored Hannah's plea for help. There was enough blame to go around.

Sharon's heart felt like lead. With the cottage and the clock gone, there was nothing to hold them together. If they were too busy to see each other when everything was normal, what reason would they have to see each other with everything destroyed? The old resentments were gone, but so were the reasons to stay in touch. What was it her father had said in her dream? Come together. His wish was lost in the winds of the storm.

A strange feeling came over Sharon, like someone was pushing the back of the recliner. Hannah and Essie got off the sofa as Sharon got out of her seat. Had they felt the same prodding as she did? The three put their arms around each other and hung on tight.

A funny tugging on the back of Sharon's neck caught her attention. Her necklace was stuck on something. She reached in to free it and found it was stuck to the other two necklaces. The three necklaces were stuck together like a ball, even as the sisters tried to back up. The color changed from gold to pink to red right before it gave a clink and the necklaces fell away from each other.

"What was that?" they asked in unison.

"Hello, girls! Thanks for calling for me."

They turned in the direction of the voice. There their father stood in his three-piece suit with a watch fob hanging from his vest pocket. His gray hair and beard gave him an

C.S. Kjar

air of distinction. He held his arms open in welcome. With squeals of joy, his girls rushed to him.

Chapter 25

Hannah

Hannah's eyes blinked in disbelief. Her father had come back! The load of family responsibilities lifted from her shoulders as she raced to him. She'd lost her mother, but at least her father was here. He was the wise one who would tell them what to do. His strong arms bolstered her spirits like no one else could.

"I don't understand, how did you know?" she asked him. "The clock didn't work."

He lifted her necklace up. "What did I tell you when I left these for you? 'Hold on to it during times of trouble.' And I told Sharon for you three to come together. When you did, I came."

Essie put her hand over her face. "But Father, why didn't you come right out and tell us what the necklaces would do."

"And spoil your discovery?" He let out a chuckle wrapped in joviality. "Your mother isn't the only schemer in the family."

Hannah didn't care. He was here now, and it was all that mattered, although they had to confess they'd destroyed the clock. "Father, the clock. It's gone. The storm ruined it. We tried to put it back together, but it didn't work. The magic was gone."

He pulled his girls toward the sofa and made them sit. He pushed the coffee table out a bit and sat on it facing them. "It wasn't the magic clock," he responded. He rubbed the palms of his hands together. "Mother Nature wanted the clock and I told her she couldn't have it. She was angry with me so she sent the strong hurricane to destroy the clock. I knew what she was planning so I went to the cottage and switched the magic clock with an identical one that held no such magic. She would think she destroyed it, and her anger would be appeased. But don't worry, the magic clock is safely back with me where it belongs."

In a voice reflecting her agitation, Essie said, "Father, why didn't you tell us? You know what we've gone through for the fake clock? Why, it almost drowned Sharon."

He patted Sharon's knee. "My brave girl who overcame her fears. I'm very proud of you." Her face turned red with the compliment. "I cannot intercede in everything. If I could, I'd have stopped the storm Mother Nature brewed up." He frowned. "She owes my girls an apology."

The thought of meeting Mother Nature had its appeal, but if she'd caused so much destruction over the clock, it was best to keep a distance from her. Hannah spoke her thoughts. "Tell her she owes us nice weather and less destruction."

Father Time gave her a one-sided shrug. "I'll tell her when I see her next." He grew serious. "I know you have one more question. Your mother's last visit." He pulled his watch from his pocket. "I can call her back for you. Shall we?"

Hannah put her hand over the watch. "Not here. At the cottage. Or what's left of it."

Essie shook her head. "But she won't be able to talk with the children. Let's do it here."

"Father, she'll be here for a day, right?"

He nodded.

"Let's bring her back there, on the beach, and later we'll use the talismans to bring her back here. We can call the kids and let her talk to them on FaceTime."

Essie's face brightened. "That's a good idea. Let's do it."

Sharon was quick to agree.

Father Time sat with his eyebrows raised. "Talismans?" Hannah smiled at him. "Trust us, Father. You'll like them."

Two hours later, as the sun neared the horizon, the four family members landed where the living room once lay. Their father's mood darkened as he surveyed the destruction of his family's home. Hannah didn't want to know what he'd do when he saw Mother Nature again. Even with his absences while she was growing up, she knew he valued his family as much as any mortal man. Any threat to them wouldn't be taken lightly.

He held out his pocket watch and set the time to three. A wisp of smoke came out of the face of it, swirling and twisting in the sea breeze. It thickened until a pillar of smoke went up and settled into the sand beside him. It solidified into their mother. She opened her arms and said, "My girls!"

Holding tightly onto something they thought they had lost, the sisters hugged their mother for minutes. Hannah was afraid to let go lest it be a dream. They huddled around her as they showed her the ruins of the cottage. As they walked among the ruins, they regaled her with the story of Sharon nearly being drowned, of being accused of being looters, and of their adventures with Elvira.

To her surprise, their mother didn't seem upset by the turn of events. She sat with them on what had been the front porch. Just like in the old days, the family faced the ocean as the clouds tumbled overhead.

Hannah pulled out a videotape poking her backside as she sat on the sand. "Mother, how on earth did you ever get mixed up with Howie Howard? Didn't you know he was a greedy, crooked developer?"

"Of course, I did. He tried to buy the land from me many times, but I said no every time, and I knew you would too. I suppose I found him to be a funny, entertaining little man. I enjoyed our verbal duels."

Hannah laughed along with her sisters.

Their mother drew a dollar sign in the sand. "You got the money out before the storm, right?"

"Hannah took care of it," Essie said with a tone of regret. "She's the smart one. She's taken care of the taxes and upkeep. You'd be proud of her."

Hannah looked at Essie who mouthed "I'm sorry." The simple apology made everything right again. The fights and the hard feelings went out with the tide.

But what should they do with the land now?

Her mother read her mind. "I was thinking this area would make a pretty park. Why don't you donate the land to the city and let them turn it into one. People need a place to sit on the beach, to swim if they want, and a place to picnic and make family memories. The land will continue to do for everyone what it did for us."

The idea was perfect, like the sunset developing across the water. The family held on to each other as the heaven's colors blended together in the clouds and on the ocean.

The land donation took nearly a year of legal manipulations and hoop-jumping, but the day came for the signing over of the deed. Beautiful weather made the outdoor ceremony a festive occasion. In front of the remains of the fireplace, a table with the appropriate paperwork was set up in the sand. City officials, reporters, and a crowd of people circled and tromped where the cottage once stood.

The mayor made a long-winded speech about the generous donation of the Time family to the citizens of

Sarasota. Cameras clicked as each sister bent to sign the documents turning over the former site of the cottage and the associated land to the city for a new park to be called the Francis Time Park.

On one end of the table, large posters showed the landscape design for the new park. The entrance would have an archway with clock faces on either pillar. A large parking lot would replace the long gravel driveway. Trees and flower beds would be planted, and the beach area would be open for picnicking and swimming. The old chimney would become part of a group pavilion available for reservations for family reunions or weddings.

As the mayor shook the sisters' hands, Hannah caught sight of Howie Howard and Elvira McKinzor in the back of the crowd looking like they were sucking lemons. They sent sneers to the sisters as they turned to leave. Hannah couldn't help but laugh at the sore losers.

As Hannah moved to greet other dignitaries present, her toe hit on something hard in the sand. Looking down, the edge of a videotape stuck through the grit. She picked it up. No doubt they'd find others when construction of the park began. As she brushed it off, she saw the special mark on it indicating it was their mother's last video, the one telling them about the clock. She put it in her purse and told Sharon to speak to the construction engineer about getting any other videos they found returned to them.

In the distance, she saw a tall distinguished gentleman in a three-piece suit with a watch fob hanging out of the breast pocket. His beaming smile portrayed a father's love for his girls. She tugged on Essie's sleeve and pointed him out. Sharon followed their gaze and saw him too. He gave them a wink as he disappeared.

Their ghost-hunting friends, Jeff, Rusty, and Clay, joined in the celebration. They offered their congratulations on making such a nice gesture. They inquired about Captain Fremont and his ghostly crew and told tales of their other paranormal adventures. After having lunch together, the men offered them a ride to the airport in their black van, but they declined, having made other plans for transportation.

Hours later after the crowd had dispersed, the sisters stood arm-in-arm looking out at the ocean. Without the cottage, the place didn't feel like home anymore. They agreed it was easy to let it go. When the park was finished, it would be full of people so Hannah's opportunity to swim alone in her own little piece of the ocean would be gone.

"Want to sleep on the beach tonight? For old times' sake?" Essie asked.

Sharon laughed. "Might not ever get the opportunity again. It's the new moon so the stars will be extra bright."

Hannah looked at her sisters. "Let's get some sand in our clothes." She kicked off her shoes and took off running. "Last one in the water is a rotten egg!"

The author spent her life searching for her life's purpose. A life-long bookworm, she spent her time with lots and lots of books. Now a retired technical writer/editor, she loves to quilt, read, and write in her home in the Pacific Northwest where she lives with her husband. Two grandsons keep her feeling young.

She has self-published several novels, one children's book, and a non-fiction book that are available on Kindle and Amazon. Her books have strong women, a touch of romance, and fun adventures sprinkled with humor.

The author's last name is pronounced "care." She hopes that's what everyone will do. Care about each other.

Other Books by C.S. Kjar:

The Treasure of Adonis

Blessings From the Wrong Side of Town

The Five Grannies Go to the Ball

Scraps of Wisdom: All I Needed to Know I Learned in Quilting Class

The Christmas Eve Wedding

The Sisters of Time Series
- o   The Secrets of the Clock, Book 1
- o   The Secrets of the Cottage, Book 2
- o   The Secrets of the Storm, Book 3

For more information:

Visit my website at https://cskjar.com

Be a friend on my Facebook page at http://www.facebook.com/cskjar.

You can also follow me on Twitter at @cskjar.

Please help me...

One of the best things you can do for an author is write a review. Please tell me what you thought of this novel by leaving a review with one or more of your favorite retailers. Even a short review, one or two lines, can be a tremendous help to me.

Your review is also a gift to other readers who may be searching for just this sort of story, and they will be grateful that you helped them find it.

If you write a review, please send me an email at cskjar.books@gmail.com so I can thank you with a personal reply.

Also, tell your friends, readers' groups, and discussion boards about this book.

Thank you very much for your support.

C.S. Kjar

C.S. Kjar

Acknowledgements

Again, thanks to my husband who has put up with me for more than four decades and supports me in my writing career. He's my biggest cheerleader.

A huge thank you and a big hug to my sister Julie. Without her help, I'd be lost.

Thanks also to all those who read through the series. Thank you for your patience in waiting for the final book. I hope you'll find it was worth the wait.

Thanks to all my readers for your encouragement. It means more than I can say.